Waterstones
Presents

The Shortlist
The Sunday Times EFG Private Bank
Short Story Award

2012

—

Six Short Stories
by Kevin Barry, Emma Donoghue, Linda Oatman High,

Jean Kwok, Tom Lee and Robert Minhinnick

Waterstones

THE SUNDAY TIMES

EFG Private Bank

Published by Waterstones Booksellers Ltd.

This is a limited edition of 5000 copies.

Waterstones would like to thank WordTheatre®: Giving Voice to Great Writing for their support organising events.

Produced by The Curved House.
Printed in the UK.

Contents

———

Introduction v

Beer Trip to Llandudno / Kevin Barry 1

———

The Hunt / Emma Donoghue 29

———

Where the Gods Fly / Jean Kwok 45

———

The Current / Tom Lee 63

———

El Aziz: Some Pages from His Notebooks /
Robert Minhinnick 91

———

Nickel Mines Hardware / Linda Oatman High 109

———

Acknowledgements 135

Introduction

All we have is the story. It gives shape to our lives. We look
for a detail to lay bare a relationship, a phrase with the power
to break the heart or make it sing; something that casts a
particular slant of light on the everyday. That's what the short
story can do: in a few thousand words it can contain all the
textured expansiveness of a novel and the lyrical intensity of a
poem. To succeed in this is no easy thing and celebrating the
very best of the art of the short story is what the The Sunday
Times EFG Private Bank Short Story Award is about. This
limited edition of the 2012 shortlist presents stories as touching,
disturbing, contrary and joyous as the human spirit itself.
Congratulations to the writers whose work has created such a
fine volume. Their efforts and imagination will be enjoyed for
years to come.

Cathy Galvin, Director
The Sunday Times EFG Private Bank Short Story Award

Biography

KEVIN BARRY was longlisted for The Sunday Times EFG Private Bank Short Story Award in 2011. His first short story collection, *There Are Little Kingdoms* (Stinging Fly Press), was published in 2007 and was awarded the Rooney Prize for Irish Literature and his second, *Dark Lies the Island* (Jonathan Cape), will be published in April. His first novel, *City of Bohane*, was published in 2011 and was shortlisted for both the Costa First Novel Award and the Hughes and Hughes Irish Novel of the Year. Kevin's stories have appeared in the *New Yorker*, the *Granta Book of the Irish Short Story* and *Best European Fiction 2011* among others, and his plays have been produced in Ireland and the US. He lives in County Sligo, Ireland.

Beer Trip to Llandudno

by

Kevin Barry

———

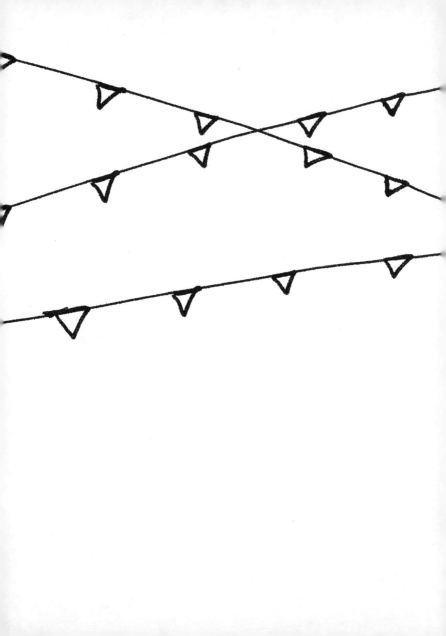

It was a pig of a day, as hot as we'd had, and we were down to our T-shirts taking off from Lime Street. This was a sight to behold – we were all of us biggish lads. It was Real Ale Club's July outing, a Saturday, and we'd had word of several good houses to be found in Llandudno. I was double-jobbing for Ale Club that year. I was in charge of publications and outings both. Which was controversial.

"Rhyl … We'll pass Rhyl, won't we?"

This was Mo.

"We'd have come over to Rhyl as kids," said Mo. "Ferry and coach. I remember the rollercoasters."

"Never past Prestatyn, me," said Tom Neresford.

Tom N – so-called; there were three Toms in Ale Club – rubbed at his belly in a worried way. There was sympathy for that. We all knew stomach trouble for a bugger.

"Down on its luck'd be my guess," said Everett Bell. "All these old North Wales resorts have suffered dreadfully, haven't they? Whole mob's gone off to bloody Laos on packages. Bloody Cambodia, bucket and spade."

Everett wasn't inclined to take the happy view of things. Billy Stroud, the ex-Marxist, had nothing to offer about Llandudno. Billy was involved with his timetables.

"Two minutes and fifty seconds late taking off," he said, as the train skirted the Toxteth estates. "This thing hits Llandudno for 1.55 p.m., I'm an exotic dancer."

3

Aigburth station offered a clutch of young girls in their summer skimpies. Oiled flesh, unscarred tummies, and it wasn't yet noon. We groaned under our breaths. We'd taken on a crate of Marston's Old Familiar for the journey, 3.9 per cent to volume. Outside, the estuary sulked away in terrific heat and Birkenhead shimmered across the water. Which wasn't like Birkenhead. I opened my *AA Illustrated Guide to Britain's Coast* and read from its entry on Llandudno:

"A major resort of the North Wales coastline, it owes its well-planned streets and promenade to one Edward Mostyn, who, in the mid 19th century – "

"Victorian effort," said John Mosely. "Thought as much."

If there was a dad figure among us, it was Big John, with his know-it-all interruptions.

"Who in the mid 19th century," I repeated, "laid out a new town on former marshland below ..."

"They've built it on a marsh, have they?" said Everett Bell.

"TB," said Billy Stroud. "Marshy environment was considered healthful."

"Says here there's water skiing available from Llandudno jetty."

"That'll be me," said Mo, and we all laughed.

Hot as pigs, but companionable, and the train was in Cheshire quick enough. We had dark feelings about Cheshire that summer. At the North West Beer Festival, in the spring, the Cheshire crew had come over a shade cocky. Just because they were chocka with half-beam pubs in pretty villages. Warrington lads were fine. We could take the Salford lot even. But the Cheshire boys were arrogant and we sniffed as we passed through their country.

"A bloody suburb, essentially," said Everett.

"Chester's a regular shithole," said Mo.

"But you'd have to allow Delamere Forest is a nice walk?" said Tom N.

Eyebrows raised at this, Tom N not being an obvious forest walker.

"You been lately, Tom? Nice walk?"

Tom nodded, all sombre.

"Was out for a Christmas tree actually," he said.

This brought gales of laughter. It is strange what comes over as hilarious when hangovers are general. We had the windows open to circulate what breeze there was. Billy Stroud had an earpiece in for the radio news. He winced:

"They're saying it'll hit 36.5," he said. "Celsius."

We sighed. We sipped. We made Wales quick enough and we raised our Marston's to it. Better this than to be stuck in a garden listening to a missus. We meet as much as five nights of the week, more often six. There are those who'd call us a bunch of sots but we don't see ourselves like that. We see ourselves as hobbyists. The train pulled into Flint and Tom N went on the platform to fetch in some beef 'n' gravies from the Pie-O-Matic.

"Just the thing," said Billy Stroud, as we sweated over our dripping punnets. "Cold stuff causes the body too much work, you feel worse. But a nice hot pie goes down a treat. Perverse, I know. But they're on the curries in Bombay, aren't they?"

"Mumbai," said Everett.

The train scooted along the fried coast. We made solid headway into the Marston's. Mo was down a testicle since the spring. We'd called in at the Royal the night of his operation. We'd stopped at the Ship and Mitre on the way – they'd a handsome bitter from Clitheroe on guest tap. We needed the fortification: when Real Ale Club boys parade down hospital wards, we tend to draw worried glances from the whitecoats. We are shaped like those chaps in the warning illustrations on cardiac charts. We gathered around Mo and breathed a nice fog of bitter over the lad and we joshed him but gently.

"Sounding a little high-pitched, Mo?"

"Other lad's going to be worked overtime."

"Diseased bugger you'll want in a glass jar, Mo. One for the mantlepiece."

Love is a strong word, but. We were family to Mo when he was up the Royal having the bollock out. We passed Flint Castle and Everett Bell piped up.

"Richard the Second," he said.

We raised eyebrows. We were no philistines at Ale Club, Merseyside branch. Everett nodded, pleased.

"This is where he was backed into a corner," he said. "By Bolingbroke."

"Boling who?"

"Bolingbroke, the usurper. Old Dick surrendered for a finish. At Flint Castle. Or that's how Shakespeare had it."

"There's a contrary view, Ev?"

"Some say it was more likely Conwy but I'd be happy with the Bard's read," he said, narrowing his eyes, the matter closed.

"We'll pass Conwy Castle in a bit, won't we?"

I consulted my *Illustrated AA.*

"We'll not," I said. "But we may well catch a glimpse across the estuary from Llandudno Junction."

There was a holiday air at the stations. Families piled on, the dads with papers, the mams with lotion, the kids with phones. The beer ran out by Abergele and this was frowned upon: poor planning. We were reduced to buying train beer, Worthingtons. Sourly we sipped and Everett came and had a go.

"Maybe if one man wasn't in charge of outings *and* publications," he said, "we wouldn't be running dry halfways to Llandudno."

"True, Everett," I said, calmly, though I could feel the colour rising in my cheeks. "So if anyone cares to step up, I'll happily step aside. From either or."

"We need you on publications, kid," said John Mosely. "You're the man for the computers."

Publications lately was indeed largely web-based. I maintained our site on a regular basis, posting beer-related news and links. I was also looking into online initiatives to attract the younger drinker.

"I'm happy on publications, John," I said. "The debacle with the newsletter aside."

Newsletter had been a disaster, I accepted that. The report on the Macclesfield outing had been printed upside down. Off-colour remarks had been made about a landlady in Everton, which should never have got past an editor's eye, as the lady in question kept very fine pumps. It hadn't been for want of editorial meetings. We'd had several, mostly down the Grapes of Wrath.

"So how's about outings then?" I said, as the train swept by Colwyn Bay. "Where's our volunteer there? Who's for the step-up?"

Everett showed a palm to placate me.

"There's nothin' personal in this, lad," he said.

"I know that, Ev."

Ale Club outings were civilised events. They never got aggressive. Maudlin, yes, but never aggressive. Rhos-on-Sea; the Penrhyn sands. We knew Everett had been through a hard time. His old dad passed on and there'd been sticky business with the will. Ev would turn a mournful eye on us, at the bar of the Lion, in the snug of the Ship, and he'd say:

"My brother got the house, my sister got the money, I got the manic depression."

Black as his moods could be, as sharp as his tongue, Everett was tender. Train came around Little Ormes Head and Billy Stroud went off on one about Ceausescu.

"Longer it recedes in the mind's eye," he said, "the more like Romania seems the critical moment."

"Apropos of, Bill?"

"Apropos my arse. As for Liverpool? Myth was piled upon myth, wasn't it? They said Labour sent out termination notices to council workers by taxi. Never bloody happened! It was an anti-red smear!"

"Thatcher's sick and old, Billy," said John Mosely.

"Aye an' her spawn's all around us yet," said Billy, and he broke into a broad smile, his humours mysteriously righted, his fun returned.

Looming, then, the shadow of Great Ormes Head, and beneath it a crescent swathe of bay, a beach, a prom, and terraces: here lay Llandudno.

"1.55 p.m.," said Everett. "On the nose."

"Where's our exotic dancer?" teased Mo.

Billy Stroud sadly raised his T-shirt above his man boobs. He put his arms above his head, slowly gyrated his vast belly and danced his way off the train. We lost weight in tears as we tumbled onto the platform.

"How much for a private session, miss?" called Tom N.

"Tenner for twenty minutes," said Billy. "Fiver, I'll stay the full half hour."

We walked out of Llandudno station and plumb into a headbutt of heat.

"Blood and tar!" I cried. "We'll be hittin' the lagers!"

"Wash your mouth out with soap and water," said John Mosely.

Big John rubbed his hands together and led the way – Big John was first over the top. He reminded us there was business to hand.

"We're going to need a decision," he said, "about the National Beer Scoring System."

Here was kerfuffle. The NBSS, by long tradition, ranked a beer from nought-to-five. Nought was take-backable, a crime against the name of ale. One was barely drinkable, two so-so, three an eyebrow raised in mild appreciation. A four was an ale on top form, a good beer in proud nick. A five was angel's tears but a seasoned drinker would rarely dish out a five, would over the course of a lifetime's quaffing call no more than a handful of fives. Such was the NBSS, as was. However, Real Ale Club, Merseyside branch, had for some time felt that the system lacked subtlety. And one famous night, down Rigby's, we came up with our own system – we marked from nought-to-ten. Finer gradations of purity were thus allowed for. The nuances of a beer were more properly considered. A certain hoppy tang, redolent of summer hedgerows, might elevate a brew from a seven to an eight. The mellow back-note born of a good oak casking might lift an ale again, and to the rare peaks of the nines. Billy Stroud had argued for decimal breakdown, for seven-point-fives and eight-point-fives – Billy would – but we had to draw a line somewhere. The national organisation responded badly. They sent stiff word down the email but we continued to forward our beer reports with markings on a nought-to-ten scale. There was talk now of us losing the charter. These were heady days.

"Stuff them is my view," said Everett Bell.

"We'd lose a lot if we lost the charter," said Mo. "Think about the festival invites. Think about the history of the branch."

"Think about the bloody future!" cried Tom N. "We haven't come up with a new system to be awkward. We've done it for the ale drinkers. We've done it for the ale makers!"

I felt a lump in my throat and I daresay I wasn't alone.

"Ours is the better system," said Everett. "This much we know."

"You're right," said John Mosely, and this was the clincher, Big John's call. "I say we score nought to ten."

"If you lot are in, that's good enough for me," I said.

Six stout men linked arms on a hot Llandudno pavement. We rounded the turn onto the prom and our first port of call: the Heron Inn.

Which turned out to be an anti-climax. A nice house, lately refurbished, but mostly keg rubbish on the taps. The Heron did, however, do a Phoenix Tram Driver on cask, 3.8 per cent, and we sat with six of same.

"I've had better Tram Drivers," opened Mo.

"I've had worse," countered Tom N.

"She has a nice delivery but I'd worry about her legs," said Billy Stroud, shrewdly.

"You wouldn't be having more than a couple," said John Mosely.

"*Not* a skinful beer," I concurred.

All eyes turned to Everett Bell. He held a hand aloft, wavered it.

"A five would be generous, a six insane," he said.

"Give her the five," said Big John, dismissively.

I made the note. This was as smoothly as a beer was ever scored. There had been some world-historical ructions in our day. There was the time Billy Stroud and Mo hadn't talked for a month over an eight handed out to a Belhaven Bombardier.

Alewards we followed our noses. We walked by the throng of the beach – the shrieks of the sun-crazed kids made our stomachs loop. We made towards the Prom View Hotel. We'd had word of a new landlord there, an ale-fancier. It was dogs-dying-in-parked-cars weather. The Prom View's ample lounge was a blessed reprieve. We had the place to ourselves, the rest of Llandudno apparently being content with summer, sea and life. John Mosely nodded towards a smashing row of hand pumps for the casks. Low whistles sounded. The landlord, hot-faced and jovial, came through from the hotel's reception.

"Another tactic," he said, "would be stay home and have a nice sauna."

"Same difference," sighed John Mosely.

"Could be looking at 37.2 now," said the landlord, taking a flop of sweat from his brow.

Billy Stroud sensed a kindred spirit:

"Gone up again, has it?"

"And up," said the landlord. "My money's on a 38 before we're out."

"Record won't go," said Billy.

"Nobody's said record," said the landlord. "We're not going to see a 38.5, that's for sure."

"Brogdale in Kent," said Billy. "August 10th, 2003."

"2.05 p.m.," said the landlord. "I wasn't five miles distant that same day."

Billy was beaten.

"Loading a van for a divorced sister," said the landlord, ramming home his advantage. "Lugging sofas in the piggin' heat. And wardrobes!"

We bowed our heads to the man.

"What'll I fetch you, gents?"

A round of Cornish Lightning was requested.

"Taking the sun?" enquired the landlord.

"Taking the ale."

"After me own heart," he said. "Course 'round here, it's lagers they're after mostly. Bloody Welsh."

"Can't beat sense into them," said John Mosely.

"If I could, I would," said the landlord, and he danced as a young featherweight might, he raised his clammy dukes. Then he skipped and turned.

"I'll pop along on my errands, boys," he said. "There are rows to hoe and socks for the wash. You'd go through pair after pair this weather."

He pinched his nostrils closed: what-a-pong.

"Soon as you're ready for more, ring that bell and my good wife will oblige. So adieu, adieu …"

He skipped away. We raised eyes. The shade of the lounge was pleasant, the Cornish Lightning in decent nick.

"Call it a six?" said Tom N.

Nervelessly we agreed. Talk was limited. We swallowed hungrily, quickly, and peered again towards the pumps.

"The Lancaster Bomber?"

"The Whitstable Mule?"

"How's about that Mangan's Organic?"

"I'd say the Lancaster all told."

"Ring the bell, Everett,"

He did so, and a lively blonde, familiar with her 40s but nicely preserved, bounced through from reception. Our eyes went shyly down. She took a glass to shine as she waited our call. Type of lass who needs her hands occupied.

"Do you for, gents?"

Irish, her accent.

"Round of the Lancaster, wasn't it?" said Everett.

She squinted towards our table, counted the heads.

"Times six," confirmed Everett.

The landlady squinted harder. She dropped the glass. It smashed to pieces on the floor.

"Maurice?" she said.

It was Mo that froze, stared, softened.

"B-B-Barbara?" he said.

We watched as he rose and crossed to the bar. A man in a dream was Mo. We held our breaths as Mo and Barbara took each other's hands over the counter. They were wordless for some moments, and then felt ten eyes on them, for they giggled, and Barbara set blushing to the Lancasters. She must have spilled half again down the slops gully as she poured. I joined Everett to carry the ales to our table. Mo and Barbara went into a huddle down the far end of the counter. They were rapt.

Real Ale Club would not have marked Mo for a romancer.

"The quiet ones you watch," said Tom N. "Maur*ice*?"

"Mo? With a piece?" whispered Everett Bell.

"Could be they're old family friends," tried innocent Billy. "Or relations?"

Barbara was now slowly stroking Mo's wrist.

"Four buggerin' fishwives I'm sat with," said John Mosely. "What are we to make of these Lancasters?"

We talked ale but were distracted. Our glances cut down the length of the bar. Mo and Barbara talked lowly, quickly, excitedly down there. She was moved by Mo, we could see that plain enough. Again and again she ran her fingers through her hair. Mo was gazing at her, all dreamy, and suddenly he'd got a thumb hooked in the belt-loop of his denims – Mr Suave. He didn't so much as touch his ale.

Next, of course, the jaunty landlord arrived back on the scene.

"Oh Alvie!" she cried. "You'll never guess!"

"Oh?" said the landlord, all the jauntiness instantly gone from him.

"This is *Maurice*!"

"Maurice?" he said. "You're joking …"

It was polite handshakes then, and feigned interest in Mo on the landlord's part, and a wee fat hand he slipped around the small of his wife's back.

"We'll be suppin' up," said John Mosely, sternly.

Mo had a last, whispered word with Barbara but her smile was fixed now and the landlord remained in close attendance. As we left, Mo looked back and raised his voice a note too loud. Desperate, he was.

"Barbara?"

We dragged him along. We'd had word of notable pork scratchings up the Mangy Otter.

"Do tell, Maur*ice*," said Tom N.

"Leave him be," said John Mosely.

"An ex, that's all," said Mo.

And Llandudno was infernal. Families raged in the heat. All of the kids wept. The Otter was busyish when we sludged in. We settled on a round of St Austell Tributes from a meagre selection. Word had not been wrong on the quality of the scratchings. And the St Austell turned out to be in top form.

"I'd be thinking in terms of a seven," said Everett Bell.

"Or a shade past that?" said John Mosely.

"You could be right on higher than sevens," said Billy Stroud. "But surely we're not calling it an eight?"

"Here we go," I said.

"Now this," said Billy Stroud, "is where your 7.5s would come in."

"We've heard this song, Billy," said John Mosely.

"He may not be wrong, John," said Everett.

"Give him a 7.5," said John Mosely, "and he'll be wanting his 6.3s, his 8.6s. There'd be no bloody end to it!"

"Tell you what," said Mo. "How about I catch up with you all a bit later? Where's next on the list?"

We stared at the carpet. It had diamonds on and crisps ground into it.

"Next up is the Crippled Ox on Burton Square," I read from my print-out. "Then it's Henderson's on Old Parade."

"See you at one or the other," said Mo.

He threw back the dregs of his St Austell and was gone.

We decided on another at the Otter. There was a Whitstable Silver Star, 6.2 per cent to volume, a regular stingo to settle our nerves.

"What's the best you've ever had?" asked Tom N.

It's a conversation that comes up again and again but it was a life-saver just then: it took our minds off Mo.

"Put a gun to my head," said Big John, "and I don't think I could look past the draught Bass I had with me dad in Peter Kavanagh's. Sixteen years of age, Friday teatime, first wage slip in my arse pocket."

"But was it the beer or the occasion, John?"

"How can you separate the two?" he said, and we all sighed.

"For depth? Legs? Back-note?" said Everett Bell. "I'd do well to ever best the Swain's Anthem I downed a November Tuesday in Stockton-on-Tees. Nineteen and '87. 4.2 per cent to volume. I was still in haulage at that time."

"I've had an Anthem," said Billy Stroud of this famously hard-to-find brew, "and I'd have to say I found it an unexceptional ale."

Everett made a face.

"So what'd be your all-time, Billy?"

The ex-Marxist knit his fingers atop the happy mound of his belly.

"Ridiculous question," he said. "There is so much wonderful ale on this island. How is a sane man to separate a Pelham High Anglican from a Warburton's Saxon Fiend? And we haven't even mentioned the great Belgian tradition. Your Duvel's hardly a dishwater. Then there's the Czechs, the Poles, the Germans ..."

"Gassy pop!" cried Big John, no fan of a German brew, of a German anything.

"Nonsense," said Billy. "A Paulaner weissbier is a sensational sup on its day."

"Where'd you think Mo's headed?" Tom N cut in.

Everett groaned:

"He'll be away down the Prom View, won't he? Big ape."

"Mo a lady-killer?" said Tom. "There's one for breaking news."

"No harm if it meant he smartened himself up a bit," said John.

"He has let himself go," said Billy. "Since the testicle."

"You'd plant spuds in those ears," I said.

The Whitstables had us in fighting form. We were away up the Crippled Ox. We found there a Miner's Slattern on cask. TV news showed sardine beaches and motorway chaos. There was an internet machine on the wall, a pound for ten minutes, and Billy Stroud went to consult the meteorological satellites. The Slattern set me pensive

Strange, I thought, how I myself had wound up a Real Ale Club stalwart. 1995, October, I'd found myself in motorway services outside Ormskirk having a screaming barny with the missus. We were moving back to her folks' place in Northern Ireland. From dratted Leicester. We were heading for the ferry at Stranraer. At services, missus told me I was an idle lardarse who had made her life hell and she never wanted to see me again. We'd only stopped off to fill the tyres. She gets in, slams the door, puts her foot down. Give her ten minutes, I thought, she'll calm down and turn back for me. Two hours later, I'm sat in an empty Chinese in services, weeping, and eating Szechuan beef. I call a taxi. Taxi comes. I says where are we, exactly? Bloke looks at me. He says Ormskirk direction. I says what's the nearest city of any size? Drop you in Liverpool for twenty quid, he says. He leaves me off downtown and I look for a pub. Spot the Ship and Mitre and in I go. I find a stunning row of pumps. I call a Beaver Mild out of Devon.

"I wouldn't," says a bloke with a beard down the bar.

"Oh?"

"Try a Marston's Old Familiar," he says, and it turns out he's Billy Stroud.

The same Billy turned from the internet machine at the Ox in Llandudno.

"37.9," he said. "Bristol Airport, a shade after three. Flights delayed, tarmac melting."

"Pig heat," said Tom N.

"We won't suffer much longer," said Billy. "There's a change due."

"Might get a night's sleep," said Everett.

The hot nights were certainly a torment. Lying there with a sheet stuck to your belly. Thoughts coming loose, beer fumes rising, a manky arse. The city beyond the flat throbbing with summer. Usually I'd get up and have a cup of tea, watch some telly. Astrophysics on Beeb Two at four in the morning, news from the galaxies, and light already in the eastern sky. I'd dial the number in Northern Ireland and then hang up before they could answer.

Mo arrived into the Ox like the ghost of Banquo. There were terrible scratch marks down his left cheek.

"A Slattern will set you right, kid," said John Mosely, discreetly, and he manoeuvred his big bones barwards.

Poor Mo was wordless as he stared into the ale that was put before him. Billy Stroud sneaked a time-out signal to Big John.

"We'd nearly give Henderson's a miss," agreed John.

"As well get back to known terrain," said Everett.

We climbed the hot streets towards the station. We stocked up with some Cumberland Pedigrees, 3.4 per cent to volume, always an easeful drop. The train was busy with daytrippers heading back. We sipped quietly. Mo looked half-dead as he slumped there but now and then he'd come up for a mouthful of his Pedigree.

"How's it tasting, kiddo?" chanced Everett.

"Like a ten," said Mo, and we all laughed.

The flicker of his old humour reassured us. The sun descended on Colwyn Bay and there was young life everywhere. I'd only spoken to her once since Ormskirk. We had details to finalise, and she was happy to let it slip about her new bloke. Some twat called Stan.

"He's emotionally spectacular," she said.

"I'm sorry to hear it, love," I said. "Given you've been through the wringer with me."

"I mean in a good way!" she barked. "I mean in a *calm* way!"

We'd a bit of fun coming up the Dee estuary with the Welsh place names.

"Fy … feen … no. Fiiiif … non … fyff … non … growy?"

This was Tom N.

"Foy. Nonn. Grewey?"

This was Everett's approximation.

"Ffynnongroew," said Billy Stroud, lilting it perfectly.
"Simple. And this one coming up? Llannerch-y-mor."

Pedigree came down my nose I laughed that hard.

"Young girl, beautiful," said Mo. "Turn around and she's
forty bloody three."

"Leave it, Mo," said Big John.

But he could not.

"She's come over early in '86. She's living up top of the
Central line, Theydon Bois. She's working in a pub there,
live-in, and ringing me from a phonebox. In Galway I'm in a
phone box too – we have to arrange the times, eight o' clock on
Tuesday, ten o'clock on Friday. It's physical fucking pain she's
not in town anymore. I'll follow in the summer is the plan and
I get there, Victoria coach station, six in the morning, eighty
quid in my pocket. And she's waiting for me there. We have an
absolute dream of a month. We're lying in the park. There's a
song out and we make it our song. 'Oh to be in England, in the
summertime, with my love, close to the edge'."

"Art of Noise," said Billy Stroud.

"Shut up, Billy!"

"Of course the next thing the summer's over and I've a start
with BT up here and she's to follow on, October is the plan.
We're ringing from phoneboxes again, Tuesdays and Fridays

but the second Friday the phone doesn't ring. Next time I see her she's forty bloody three."

Flint station we passed through, and then Connah's Quay.

"Built up, this," said Tom N. "There's an Aldi, look? And that's a new school, is it?"

"Which means you want to be keeping a good two hundred yards back," said Big John.

We were horrified. Through a miscarriage of justice, plain as, Tom N had earlier in the year been placed on a sex register. Oh the world is mad! Tom N is a placid, placid man. We were all six of us quiet as the grave on the evening train then. It grew and built, it was horrible, the silence. It was Everett at last that broke it; we were coming in for Helsby. Fair dues to Everett.

"Not like you, John," he said.

Big John nodded.

"I don't know where that came from, Tom," he said. "A bloody stupid thing to say."

Tom N raised a palm in peace but there was no disguising the hurt that had gone in. I pulled away into myself. The turns the world takes – Tom dragged through the courts, Everett half mad, Mo all scratched up and one-balled, Big John jobless for eighteen months. Billy Stroud was content, I suppose, in Billy's own way. And there was me, shipwrecked in Liverpool. Funny, for a while, to see 'Penny Lane' flagged up on the buses, but it wears off.

And then it was before us in a haze. Terrace rows we passed, out Speke way, with cook-outs on the patios. Tiny pockets of glassy laughter we heard through the open windows of the carriage. Families and what-have-you. We had the black hole of the night before us – it wanted filling. My grimmest duty as publications officer was the obits page of the newsletter. Too many had passed on at 44, at 46.

"I'm off outings," I announced. "And I'm off bloody publications as well."

"You did volunteer on both counts," reminded Big John.

"It would leave us in an unfortunate position," said Tom N.

"For my money, it's been a very pleasant outing," said Billy Stroud.

"We've supped some quality ale," concurred Big John.

"We've had some cracking weather," said Tom N.

"Llandudno is quite nice, really," said Mo.

Around his scratch marks an angry bruising had seeped. We all looked at him with tremendous fondness.

"Tis nice," said Everett Bell. "If you don't run into a she-wolf."

"If you haven't gone ten rounds with Edward bloody Scissorshands," said John Mosely.

We came along the shabby grandeurs of the city. The look on Mo's face then couldn't be read as anything but happiness.

"Mau*rice*," teased Big John, " is thinking of the rather interesting day he's had."

Mo shook his head.

"Thinking of days I had years back," he said.

It has this effect, Liverpool. You're not back in the place five minutes and you go sentimental as a famine ship. We piled off at Lime Street. There we go: six big blokes in the evening sun.

"There's the Lion Tavern?" suggested Tom N.

"There's always the Lion," I agreed.

"They've a couple of Manx ales guesting at Rigby's," said Everett Bell.

"Let's hope they're an improvement on previous Manx efforts," said Billy Stroud.

"There's the Grapes?" tried Big John.

"There's always the Grapes," I agreed.

And alewards we went about the familiar streets. The town was in carnival: Tropic of Lancashire in a July swelter. It would not last. There was rain due in off the Irish Sea, and not for the first time.

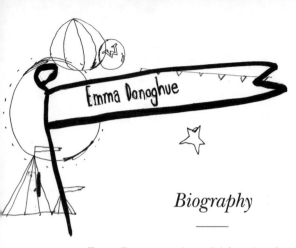

Emma Donoghue

Biography

EMMA DONOGHUE is an Irish writer born in 1969, whose fiction includes *Slammerkin, Life Mask, Touchy Subjects, The Sealed Letter* and *Room* (all Virago and Picador), which was shortlisted for the 2011 Man Booker and Orange Prizes. Her new short-story collection, *Astray,* which includes her shortlisted story 'The Hunt', is being published in October by Picador. Emma studies for her BA at University College Dublin, before moving to England to earn a PhD from the University of Cambridge. She settled in Ontario in 1998, where she lives with her partner Chris and two children, although they have spent the last year in France.

The Hunt

by

Emma Donoghue

———

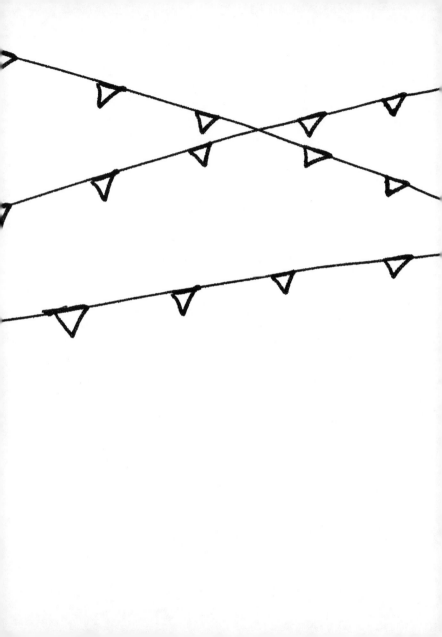

He's fifteen, or thereabouts. He thought he would be home by Christmas. That was what they were told, when they were given their red coats and shipped across the ocean to put down the rebs: that it wouldn't take more than a couple of months. But it's December already, and in New Jersey the snows are as dense as cake, and he thinks now that every soldier is told that: *home soon*. He wonders whether it's ever been true.

If the boy were in a German regiment, he could speak his own tongue at least. None of the English have even heard of Anhalt-Zerbst, let alone his village. He's never been to Hesse but his bunkmate says *you Hessians* anyway, or *you Bosch bastards*. Another points out that he's a foot or two short of a full one, so they settle on Half-Bosch.

Not soon, then, but how much longer? The redcoats took hard losses at Fort Mercer, but cleaned out Fort Lee at the end of November. The rats are in retreat, and it's this regiment's job to squeeze them out of New Jersey. There's a line of the men of Hopewell outside the garrison every morning, wanting to sign allegiance papers – not that it proves much. Washington's reb army couldn't have held together on its flight to Pennsylvania if this countryside weren't riddled with traitors, making muskets and shot for the rebs, supplying them with cloth for their backs and salt for their meat.

Some of this regiment have wives near their time, others say their wives are too pretty to leave alone; they all gripe about the endlessness of this campaign. The boy has only his mother. In the night, under the blanket, he thinks of his bed at home in his village in Anhalt-Zerbst, and the way the fir tips tap against his window, and he weeps till he shakes. His bunkmate mutters, "Give that little worm of yours a rest."

Filthy talk is how they pass the time. In the freezing rains of December there's nothing to do but wait.

Then one day the skies clear. The land around Hopewell is as hard as a drum. "Good hunting weather," somebody says.

So the hunt is what they call it. The Major isn't happy, but the Captain only shakes his head and tells him, *the men must have a bit of fun.*

Houghton and Byrne and Williams and the boy start at a farmhouse on the edge of town. Muskets at the ready in case they flush out any rebs. The boy's stomach is tight, as on the verge of battle. Nobody answers the door until Byrne smashes the fanlight with his bayonet. Then they hear running feet, and the bar lifting. Byrne grabs the maid by her skirts but Williams says "Hold hard, man. Where's your mistress, eh? Where's everybody hiding?"

She shakes her head, already sobbing.

Emma Donoghue

The boy edges to one side.

"Where are you off to, Half-Bosch?"

"Search the house?"

"That's a lad," says Houghton, undoing his buttons one by one.

Upstairs the corridors are silent, except for the creakings his steps make. Far below him he can hear dull voices, then screaming that stops all at once. The boy peers into each room, taking his time. What will he do if he finds the ladies? *Yankee whores, reb whores.*

He goes down the back stairs. In the kitchen he eats a pickle from a jar; it's weaker than his mother's, it hardly tastes at all. He strokes the grain of an old settle, reads a sampler on the wall: *Her Price Is Above Rubies.*

Something clinks. He follows the small sound into the pantry, which seems to be empty, until he opens a small door and finds a girl crouching in the meat-safe. Her hands fly to her ears.

"Monkey," he says under his breath.

"That's hardly civil!"

He points. "Hands on ears? Like the monkey in the picture."

She lowers her hands reluctantly. "Which picture?" Pale ears jut through her gleaming hair.

Like a pixie, he thinks. "Hear no bad."

"Oh, hear no evil, I see." She's crawling out and standing up, taller than he was expecting. A shiny apron, the kind that's just for show; a locket on a ribbon. "You're not English," she says accusingly.

"*Nein.*" He only slips when he's flustered.

"A mercenary!" Like something rotten in her mouth. The boy must be looking blank, because she explains: "You serve for pay, for money."

"No money," he tells her. "I get my coat. Boots. Rations."

Which reminds him to examine the shelves. He finds a basket, grabs some jars, a cake in paper, the first dark bottle his hand falls on.

"Then what brings you all the way in New Jersey?" she asks, close behind him.

"My Prince sold me. To the redcoats." He crams three more bottles in on top of the cake.

"How could he sell you, when you're as white as me?" scoffs the girl. And then, "That's my aunt's best cherry brandy you're stealing."

"Requisitioning," he says, tripping over the English syllables.

"Half-Bosch!" The voice is Byrne's, faint but getting nearer.

The boy shoots out of the pantry with his basket. "Drink," he roars, "I found drink." He doesn't have time to look back.

He thinks about her, though. That night, in the barracks, when men are swapping dirty stories, and Williams and Houghton and Byrne are going on and all about the maid at the deserted farm – the boy pretends the brandy has put him to sleep. He squeezes his eyes shut and thinks of those pearly, sticking-out ears.

There's a rumour going round that Washington's reb army will melt away on New Year's Day, when the terms of service for most of his recruits come to an end. The boy tries to imagine being home for the spring planting.

The next day the hunt is on again. The redcoats trawl through Hopewell. There are scarlet ribbons on almost every door by now, but ribbon's cheap; it says loyalty, without proving it. They knock on every door, and shout "Bring out your females!" The boy stands guard outside the surgery while the others are inside with the doctor's wife and daughter. After half an hour Williams sticks his head out the window to say "Come on it, Half-Bosch, time we made a man of you."

He pulls a face. "Still sick from the damn brandy."

Williams grins and bangs the window shut so hard that an icicle falls like a spear.

"Let's go back to the farm," Houghton proposes that night. "I hate the thought of leaving a single maidenhead in the fucking State of New Jersey."

Williams laughs so hard he coughs.

In morning the fields crack like glass under the soldiers' boots. The boy doesn't want to be walking this way again, and he wants it more than anything.

They get there in half an hour, and this time they go round to the backdoor: a stealth attack.

But the place is deserted; no sign of the maid, even. The three Englishmen troop upstairs, and the boy heads for the pantry.

The girl's there, as he knew she'd be. She has some cheese for him; it's surprisingly strong. He finds himself telling her about the day he cut a purse from a gentleman's belt, back in Anhalt-Zerbst.

"I knew you were a thief."

He shrugs. "You're a reb."

"I am not!" Too loud for the narrow pantry. "I'm as loyal as you like. I never asked to come to this nest of traitors." Her hands shoot up to cup her ears.

Two feet away, he watches the tears brim along her lashes.

"My father was in the cavalry," she tells him. "So the rebs confiscated our farm in Pennsylvania, turned us out with only bedding and a plate each. Said my little brother had to stay to join their Patriot Army." Her voice skids. "Mamma sent us three elder girls off to relations, to be safe. She didn't know my aunt in Hopewell was a turncoat. And my cousins," she says, almost spitting; "they treat me like a rag to wipe their fingers on. They grudge me my dinner, won't lend me so much as a petticoat – "

His heart thumps dully in his chest. "Where are they hiding? Your aunt and cousins?"

Her pupils contract. "I don't know. A long way away," she says, without conviction.

"When did they leave?"

She shrugs. Her hands creep up through her hair.

He shocks himself by taking them in his. "Pretty ears. Don't cover them."

"You're making fun."

He shakes his head fervently. "Beautiful."

She finds him an apple. A knife to peel it. A slice for him, a slice for her. When he tries to kiss her, she pulls away, but slowly. Should he have asked first? Should he have insisted?

"Tell me where they are, these cousins who treat you so badly," he says, instead.

"It's just the elder girl, really."

"The men – the others in my company – they want women." He flushes, absurdly.

Her fingertips are pressing her ears to her head again, as if to stop them flying away.

"I must bring some women. You understand? Not you."

He thought she might weep, but she only looks into her lap. She says something, very low.

"What's that?"

"In the hayloft," she says, still whispering.

What he tells Williams and Houghton and Byrne, when he finds them upstairs filling their packs with silver plate, is that he heard voices in the barn. Williams whacks him on the back so hard it hurts. "We've got ourselves a good little hunting dog," he tells the others. "Bosch bloodhounds can't be beat."

In the barn, the boy is the last up the ladder. A child wails in the lap of a greying lady; a tall girl shrinks behind her. "Well, well, well," cries Houghton, rubbing his hands like some villain on a stage.

The aunt straightens up. "If it please you, sir – "

"Oh, you're going to please me well enough, madam, you're going to please every one of us."

Williams whoops at that.

"And anyone who puts up a fuss will get her ears cut off."

The boy hangs back. Mutters something about going for drink.

"Come, now, for the glory of the regiment," says Byrne, grabbing him by the elbow. "Fire away! Which d'you fancy – fresh meat or well aged?"

The older lady's eyes are as gray as his mother's. He wrenches himself out of Byrne's grasp, almost falls as he scrambles down the ladder.

The thing seems to go on for hours. He waits at the door of the barn, shivering in his thin red jacket.

That night he's the butt of the whole barracks. The Captain puts his thumb on the boy's collarbone. "What's this I hear? Can't raise the regimental colours for the glory of King George?"

The boy doesn't know what the right answer is.

"Last chance, Half-Bosch," announces Houghton. "Tomorrow, the Major's off to Princeton for three days, so we're going to bring the tastiest fillies in Hopewell back to the garrison. If you don't produce some manner of female and show us you know how to put her through her paces…"

"The point is," says the Captain, leaning in, breath fragrant with gin, "are you a girl or a man?" His grip shifts from collarbone to throat. "No two ways about it, Half-Bosch. Man or girl."

"I had one already," says the boy, pulling away in a fury of terror. "At the farm. I found her the first day. Much prettiest."

"Oo, keeping the best for yourself, you rat!" Byrne cackles and smacks his shoulder. "Well, bring her back tomorrow and show us what you're made of."

What he's made of? It's not a phrase the boy has heard before; it makes him think of the gingerbread boy, who ran and ran until the fox snapped him up.

He wakes before dawn and lies like a corpse. He can't feel his feet. He finds himself thinking of his mother's softly creased hands, setting down a bowl of borscht before him. He shoves the memory away. His mother would not know him. He sees as clear as lightning that he will never go home.

By noon he's kneeling beside the girl in the pantry, holding onto her hands. He tries not to hear the shouting in the distance.

"They hate me," she says again.

"How do they know it was – "

"They don't, they hated me before. But now they hate me because I wasn't in the hayloft. My aunt's demented." Her pupils are huge and dark. "The little one's not twelve. I never thought – "

"I wasn't there," he whispers, eyes down. *Yankee whores, rebel whores.*

"She's been bleeding all night."

The distant voices are rising. Clarity seizes him. "You come with me now," he says, jerking his head in the direction of the fields.

"Run away with you? Are you mad? I couldn't dream of it," she says, but her face is bright.

She's misunderstood him, but he sees his chance; he leans in and kisses her. It's not what he was expecting; lighter, more feathery. "You're my girl," he says, then, in a deep voice.

"I barely know you," she says.

She's smiling so widely that he knows he's won, and something sinks in his chest. "I won't go without you," he says.

"But my aunt, my – Where are you going?"

He hesitates. "Who knows?"

"They'll catch you. Won't they?"

He manages a shrug. He gets to his feet, not letting go of her hand.

"Let me run upstairs and pack my trunk…"

The boy shakes his head, alarmed at the thought of having to carry such a thing. "No time, little monkey. Just your coat."

Outside, panting from the hurry, she's daunted by the icy fields. "Don't you have anything for me to ride?"

"I'll lift you over the puddles," he offers.

The girl laughs. "I can jump them."

And for a moment, as they set off across the meadow hand in hand like children, he lets himself believe that they are running away. That he is man enough to be a deserter. That there's anywhere he could take this girl, without being tracked down and sent back to Hopewell in chains and hanged in front of his company. That he could bring her all the way home with him to taste his mother's borscht.

But all the while he knows how it's going to be. He will lead her into the barracks that must be already filling up with other girls, girls with torn sleeves and bloody noses and scalps, reb girls and loyal, girls whose eyes will tell this girl all she needs to know. When the Captain claps and orders Half-Bosch to fire away, this girl will start to scream, and the boy will reach down with frozen fingers and undo his buttons one by one.

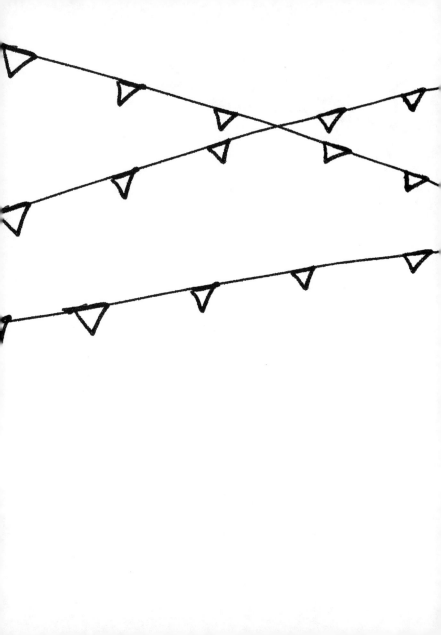

Jean Kwok

Biography

JEAN KWOK immigrated from Hong Kong to
Brooklyn when she was five and worked in
a Chinatown clothing factory for much of
her childhood. She won early admission to
Harvard, where she worked as many as four
jobs at a time, and graduated with honours
in English and American literature, before
going on to earn an MFA in Fiction at
Columbia University. In between her degrees,
Jean worked as a professional dancer for a
major ballroom dance studio for three years.
Her debut novel *Girl in Translation* (Penguin)
became a *New York Times* bestseller, has been
published in 16 countries and was named an
Orange New Writers title. Jean lives in the
Netherlands with her husband and two sons.

Where the Gods Fly
by
Jean Kwok

———

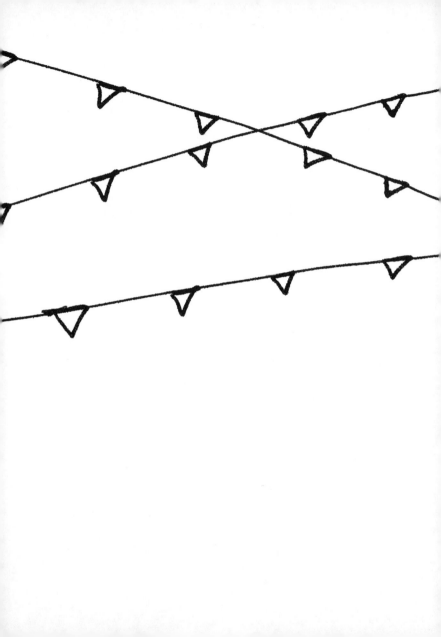

I kneel here before the gods and the thought of what I am about to do stings my eyes like incense.

I can already hear the protest from Pearl's ballet teachers – "you can't do this, she is an extraordinary talent." The gods give with one hand and take with the other, I think, and then, ashamed, immediately touch my forehead to the ground before the triple Buddhas. The gods must forgive my lack of insight. But how could those teachers understand that we had originally allowed Pearl to dance only because we had no place else to put her? Her father and I spent our waking hours at the factory in Chinatown. Pearl was too young, or so I argued, to breathe in that clogged air, thick with fabric dust that clung to our skin like a veil, turning even our sweat the colour of the garments we worked on. And somehow the consequences of that initial instinct to protect her have branched out through the years, sprouting and twisting, to arrive at this moment.

I suppose I spoiled her but she is my only girl. And she seemed so tiny when we first came to America, bundled into her red sweater and sent off to second grade alone. "Teacher doesn't like me, Mama," she would say, "teacher likes the boy with hair so white he looks like an egg. Why does teacher like egg-boy better than me?" There were never papers from school for me to see as there had been in China, where she'd brought me tests and homework filled with 100s. "Where are they?" I asked her here and the answer was always, "We didn't get any today" or "I lost them." One day, I found the pile stacked under her underwear, sheet after sheet slashed with red X's. "I didn't know we had to circle the green things," she said, pointing to one page. "Teacher took it from me and marked it all wrong before I understood what she said." This was my Pearl who had already learned to multiply and could read a Chinese newspaper.

In the beginning, we tried to leave her alone at home after school. I had no one in this country, relative or neighbour, to look after her and we could not spare a moment from the work at the factory. It's only for a few hours, I told myself, and she knows not to play with the stove and such, but I could not stand coming home to see her little face in the window of the dark apartment. "I count the headlights passing until you come home," she said. "Today there were twenty-eight. And when you don't come fast, I beat on Fat Boy until you come." Fat Boy was the stuffed dog her father had given her, one of the few toys we'd brought for her from China.

On the third day we left her alone, I found her huddled on the dusty stairs outside the apartment and when, clutching her to me, I scolded her for leaving the safety of our home, she said, "I thought I saw a face in the bathroom wallpaper and maybe it was a ghost like in the story you told me." After that, I brought her to the factory with us.

Ah, Amitabha, Buddha of great compassion, I whisper, help her to understand that all I have done, I have done because it was the only choice I had.

There were other children at the factory, of course, faces shining from the heat of the steam presses, heads already bowed by necessity and want. These were children who would grow up to wait tables in an uncle's restaurant, perhaps, or to be a fishmonger, sanding scales off carp day after day. When I looked upon Pearl at the factory, idly playing with a few spools the seamstresses had laid aside, it was as if I saw her entire life pulled taut before her like thread – her thin fingers worn callused and red by years of sewing in the factory, then, if she was lucky, marriage to some office clerk, a pack of children, and finally, Pearl the woman submerged under the struggle to feed and clothe them all. I constantly entertained hopes of Pearl's escape from the factory – if only we could afford a tutor for her, I thought, or a babysitter.

Even when she slowly, awkwardly, began to make friends and her classmates would occasionally ask her to play at their houses, we couldn't allow her to go. I understood nothing of these people who did not bow to our gods and ate with sharp knives at the table. Furthermore, we would have to invite them to visit in return; how could I serve tea with coconut slivers and sugared lotus roots in our stained apartment? "Our home is beautiful,

Mama," Pearl would say, "look at the dances the sun does in the window" but she was too little to care about the floor strewn with the mattresses we slept on, the scraps we'd brought home from the factory to cover the worn table. I had to shake out Pearl's clothes each morning to make sure no roaches had crawled in during the night. She was terrified of insects and they tormented her, antennaed heads peeking from cracks in the wall. I think the roaches were the only piece of our poverty she understood.

So it seemed a blessing when a ballet school came to give a special lesson for her third grade class and plucked Pearl out to be one of their scholarship students. Now she would have a place to go after school, at least for a few afternoons a week. I had known my child was no beauty: skinny legs sticking out from under her hand-sewn dresses and eyes too big for her face, so no one was more surprised than I when they told me they saw a great gift for ballet in her.

"But Pearl has never danced a step in her life," I protested and they said (so Pearl translated for me), "At this age, it does not matter. She's flexible and quick, her proportions are perfect and so are her feet." Later, I had puzzled over Pearl's feet. They looked as they always had, small and arched, the little toes wiggling in unison as if they were attached to each other.

When Pearl asked me in her child's vanity, "Am I pretty, Mama?" I would hesitate, and then answer, "Well, you have nice eyebrows," because I didn't want to be unkind to the girl. They are the only fine thing in her face, her eyebrows, dark and winged as a swallow against the sky. Now, a mother must not praise her child too much anyway lest the gods grow jealous but I have to say that I never could see the classical beauty these ballet people speak of so generously. The women from my family have always been small, plump, and fair, like wedding pastries powdered with flour, but even now, Pearl's cheekbones protrude, her nose is narrow and straight with no meat on it, her skin is tanned like a field worker's, and her arms and legs are as long and thin as a young man's. She is dear to me because I am her mother, but to another Chinese, she is homely indeed.

When we first came to the United States, Pearl had seemed so conspicuous in her foreignness: her shock of black hair and tawny skin in a classroom of pale freckled children. Even in China, she'd been an intense, quiet child, but here, she seemed to edge ever further inward. Gone were the rare, glad moments of laughter, Pearl twinkling up the stairs with quick light steps, suddenly erupting into a handful of cartwheels across the floor ("You'll fall on your head and your head will sink into your stomach like a turtle," I'd scold.)

And I, I was able to give her so little of myself, with the factory all day and the sewing I brought home at night, the demands constantly upon me – for rice, for clean trousers, for a pair of ears to listen. Why it should be that those who demand are the ones who receive, I do not know, but so it was with us. Even though Pearl would tug at my skirt beside every hot dog cart we passed in the street, never daring to ask but yearning with her eyes, I could count on the fingers of my left hand the number of times I actually bought one for her. Pearl as a child loved all kinds of food: marinated chicken claws, ginger fish, sweet dumplings, pizza. There was no money then to waste on such frivolities but how many times since have I wished that I'd managed to squeeze out a little more for my youngest. Now, when I try to urge a bit more food upon her, it's always "No, thank you, Ma."

Perhaps it was after she began to dance that she developed that luminous quality people praise. Even I have seen it, but only when she is performing, when she seems as cloaked by her dazzling grace as she is by her solitude off the stage.

After Pearl began to take classes at the ballet school as one of their honoured scholarship students, she became suddenly popular. Mothers who had only glanced at me to look over my simple clothes were now eager to smile as they passed us. People began to tell me what a lovely child Pearl was and how beautiful a woman she would grow up to be. But how could I trust people such as this? Perhaps they place the tall hat of flattery on your head while they're actually laughing when you turn your face away. This is wisdom my mother passed onto me and this is what I said to Pearl when she, blushing, would translate their words.

Although I didn't have to pay a dime for her dance classes, it was a great expense to pay so much for a pair of leather ballet shoes and the one set of leotard and tights, which Pearl washed every night in the yellowed bathroom sink. When her father objected, I reminded him Pearl's teacher in the regular school had told us that dancing would help her get into university later on. Now, I myself do not understand how that could be, but who am I to argue with the teacher?

In private, though, I took Pearl aside and said, "Dancing is not something you can keep, like food, or a house, or a university diploma. A few minutes, an hour, and it is gone. If you had an education, you wouldn't have to be dependent on your husband." But she did not listen. When I was a girl in China, I was not permitted to go to classes. Much of the learning I possess, I picked up through lingering at the table, pretending to dust or sweep, as my brothers studied. My mother, a progressive woman, knew what I was doing and not only allowed me this but would leave their books where I could find them when no one else was home. I suppose I left Pearl too much alone in those early years. She had nothing to hold on to, nothing that was hers, and so she never learned the value of such things.

As the years passed, she began to take classes every day, rushing breathless to the factory to help us out for an hour or two afterwards, her heavy dance bag biting into her narrow shoulder. It was as if the ballet school had swallowed her into its muscled belly; she seemed to belong to a world so foreign to the factory by then that I no longer even minded her presence there.

The glory of her dancing passed into her life at school. At first, I was pleased because she did better in her classes and she seemed to smile more. But slowly, instead of quietly studying or reading, she started to spend her free time on the phone. Suddenly popular, she was invited to movies, get-togethers, holiday dinners. I agreed with her father, of course, that she could not be allowed to go out with her friends as befitted a proper Chinese girl. Once, after we again denied permission for some longed-for dance or party, I heard her sobbing through the sound of running water in the bathroom. The bathroom was the only place she could be alone and she stayed in it for hours. She used to keep everyone at a certain distance; soon, it was only her family she kept away – she embraced the American world now that it embraced her.

When I heard her talking and laughing on the telephone with her American friends, jabbering in English much faster than she could speak Chinese by then, a part of me wanted to run over and wrench the phone from her hands. She could have been giggling over anything – boys, drinking – how could I know? It was just babble to me, her own mother, who used to hold Pearl in my lap and tell her of the fiery Dragon Kings who ruled the seas, the heavenly kingdom turned upside down by a monkey born from a stone egg. After reading her the story of a boy whose father was eaten by a tiger, I'd looked up to find her small face wet with tears. And for years it had been little Pearl who had gone everywhere with me to act as my ears and tongue; she'd told me the prices of cabbage and fruit, spoken for me at the bank, shown me where to buy women's undergarments.

I tell you the truth now, that I wanted to learn English, wanted to learn it for my daughter more than for anything else, because how could I truly be a mother to my youngest when everything she said was a mystery to me? But English was too hard for me, and for her father too.

I should perhaps have stopped Pearl from dancing sooner but I had so little else to give her. Anyway, her father began to sicken when she was almost fourteen, and I had enough else on my mind.

The female monks behind me have started to beat on the prayer drums. I stand up and move to the back of the room, where a line has already started to form for walking meditation or "walking the winds of fate," as we call it. It is not easy to maintain your balance when the winds of fate blow upon your back; when they are strong, if you are not as strong as they, they can topple you over and roll you into the earth. But if you have the strength to withstand their blows, they can propel you to where the gods fly. Pearl once told me that in the West, there is an old story of three sisters who spin and cut the thread of life.

"Chinese," I replied, "must be stronger than that; we have the responsibility of choosing our own fate because we pick which winds to walk with, or to fight against."

"But aren't some winds too strong to resist?" she asked.

"Yes," I said, "but it is not for us to decide which those are. To be human is to choose until we can choose no more."

As I circle the room led by the drumming of the monks, I begin to pray to the spirit of her father. *Ah Sun, why did you leave us so fast? We still have need of you: especially now, your daughter, whom you would call "Little Rabbit" because she was so quick to fetch your things. Do you still remember that in your land of shadows? Help us turn these winds of fate around.*

The evil winds had begun to foment around the time Pearl was in eighth grade, when she auditioned for that other ballet school, the legendary one. The greatest ballerinas trained there, she said, and their professional dance company was one of the best in the world.

I worried that her old dance school might think she was disloyal for trying to get admitted into another but she had only shrugged. "If I do get in, they'll be thrilled. And the number of students they get will double." "Do so many Americans want to be ballet dancers?" I asked then and Pearl had laughed. If she could go to a better ballet school, I thought, well, why not?

I remember that audition clearly: waiting in the packed room for hours before it was Pearl's turn, the parents and children eyeing each other to see who was better trained, more talented, more beautiful. Pearl had never looked more vulnerable to me, with her ribs poking through the thin material of the leotard, the number pinned to her chest like the sheet of magic paper the gods paste on a mountain to contain the demons within. She seemed totally unaware of anyone but the three judges, looking neither to the left nor the right, as though she were under a spell.

Before any of the twelve girls were allowed to dance a step, one judge, the tall woman with the red hair, went down the line and picked up each girl's leg and raised it as high as it would go. In front, to the side, in back – and as she did this, she felt the hip joint with her long thin hands, while the other two took notes and spoke to each other in Russian. When she came to Pearl, I was afraid for my girl, although I cared nothing for this ballet school. But Pearl's leg went higher than anyone else's, her small arched foot almost reaching her eyebrows – I've seen it fly higher since, but she was only fourteen at the time.

Immediately after this, although the girls hadn't moved an inch from the bar, five of them were asked to leave the room. The judges were already finished with them. As I moved aside to let those girls pass through the doorway, I thought to myself, these judges are people with no compassion; it has been carved out and replaced with discipline, muscle, and bone.

I'd always been too busy with work to spare time for most of Pearl's recitals and when I did go, there'd been the constant struggle to keep myself awake through my exhaustion. It was at that audition that I truly paid attention to Pearl's dancing for the first time. I saw her standing in the corner waiting for her turn to do the combination and I suddenly wanted to gather her in my arms and flee the room, flee these people. We don't belong here, I wanted to say, what do we simple Chinese know of these inhuman people with their impassive faces and elegant shoulders?

But then Pearl stepped onto the floor and I no longer recognized my daughter. Every glance, every limb, the arch of her hand, curve of leg, was suspended in beauty and a terrible poignancy. She flew, she turned and leapt like water in motion, weightless and infinitely powerful. She had been made of stone and now was freed. I felt suddenly dizzy – was this then, what had been happening while I cooked rice, folded the sheets, worked the sewing machine? When had this change, this great gift, come upon my daughter? The room was hushed after Pearl's turn. Then the red-haired woman gave a little smile.

Pearl was offered a full scholarship. Her old ballet school was as happy as she had predicted. When I urged her to translate my apologies to the principal for our ingratitude in leaving it, he protested, "No, no, it is a great honour for us. No one in the history of our school has ever been offered such a thing."

In the years she danced for that school, I was busy trying to keep her father with us, feeding him boiled fish intestines and octopus limbs for nourishment, crushed salted bumblebees for his constant cough.

In China, people died of evil spirits, curses, and old age; here, they call it cancer. Does it matter? Truth has as many visages as the god with infinite faces who can see in every direction. But in the end, the faces are all one: we lost her father.

The monks are ringing the gong. As I gather my things to go, I pause for a moment by the window where the setting sun dances upon the glass.

Everything has been blown by the winds of fate; here I am in America, my husband has just died, and my daughter is pursuing something too ephemeral to grasp. I have let the winds take us where they will for too long; now, I act upon my choice. Please, great Buddhas, allow my daughter to understand some day why I take her greatest love away; I know this will be the blow that finally severs the already tenuous bonds between us. I will go to Pearl now. She is not yet seventeen – time enough to follow another path, to look upon another face of the god. It is my fault that it has all come to this; I have been a foolish, doting mother.

She can go to the local school, perhaps she could study accounting or dentistry. Then she will have something substantial to cling to when I am no longer here to look after her. There is no one else now. She said to me once, "Ma, it all passes anyway," but it is only human to try to keep, to hold and to love.

She is gifted and she is stunning on stage, I know, but these things are not for such as us. We who have lost everything – our country, our family, our culture – cannot afford to be exceptional. To have enough to live by, to eat, that is enough. And someday, if she proves to be strong enough, let her then stand before the wind like incense that threads through the air: turning, swirling, searching for the place where the gods fly.

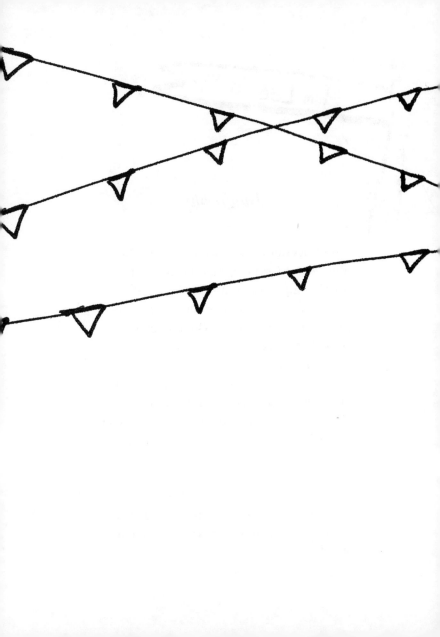

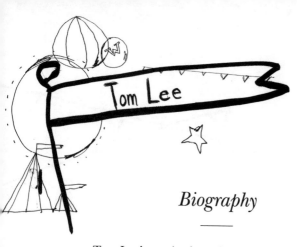

Tom Lee

Biography

TOM LEE's stories have been published in
the *Sunday Times Magazine, Prospect* and
Esquire, broadcast on BBC Radio 4 and
two are being adapted for film. In 2004 he
received an Arts Council Grant to finish
his debut collection, *Greenfly* (Harvill
Secker) which was published in 2009. In
2007 his story 'The Good Guy' was runner-
up in the Royal Society of Literature's V.S.
Pritchett Memorial Prize. He has performed
readings throughout the country, taught
literature and creative writing at Goldsmiths
College and the Open University, and
provided editorial advice for The Literary
Consultancy. He is currently working on a
second collection of stories and completing
a PhD at Goldsmiths College.

The Current
by
Tom Lee

———

Ever since my father's treatment – which, in many ways, had to be considered a success – it had been hard to know what to do with him. My brother and I went to pick him up from the farmhouse in Dorset where he had been staying for the week. When we pulled into the driveway we could see him sitting around a table in the garden with seven or eight others, all talking and smiling, their faces turned to receive the sun which was bright and high in the sky. He came over to the car, hugged us both fiercely – uncharacteristically so – and then led us over to the group. "These are my boys," he said to them, and then told us everyone's names. Someone brought us tea from inside the house and a balding young man in a yellow t-shirt began to ask me a series of earnest questions, about my work, my family, my plans for the future. Next to me, my brother was receiving the same treatment from someone else. Meanwhile, my father seemed to have resumed telling a story, the details of which I could not catch but which was punctuated by comments and bursts of laughter from the rest of the group. Altogether, an air of brittle hilarity, or even joy, hung over the scene and in this – as in other ways – they struck me as resembling nothing so much as a group of hostages suddenly and unexpectedly given their freedom.

After ten minutes or so my father finished his story, stood up and began to embrace each person around the table. There were vows to email and phone and get together again soon, emotional goodbyes that seemed excessive for people who had known each other for not even a week. My brother and I found ourselves shaking hands with each member of the group in turn, accepting their good wishes. Before we got in the car, my father made a great show of folding up his wheelchair and packing it in the boot.

In the car, my father talked – very rapidly, a stream of free association, flitting from one subject to another, the words sometimes getting tangled up or muddled, his mind apparently moving more quickly than he could articulate. He sat in the back, his face pressed against the window, pointing out everything that went past, a vintage car similar to one his brother had once owned, a pub that would have been nice for lunch except it was past lunchtime and anyway he wasn't hungry, repeatedly marvelling at the loveliness of the day and the countryside, the hills, the blossom on the trees, how all this made him think of a holiday he and my mother had taken nearby before my brother and I were born. Throughout this, one of his feet drummed rapidly on the floor of the car.

My brother asked him what they had done during the week, the nature of the treatment, but he would not be drawn on details. "Amazing people, just amazing people," he said, although it was not clear if he was referring to those we had been introduced to in the garden – his fellow hostages – or others who had remained unseen. "Don't worry, you'll hear all about it," he said, although somehow we never did. At times he seemed exhausted by his own efforts. He would try and stop himself, closing his eyes and taking deep breaths, one hand placed across his chest, as if swearing an oath. At one point he took a small card from his wallet and began to mouth whatever was written on it, some kind of mantra perhaps, but then something else caught his attention beyond the car window and he was talking again.

After an hour we stopped at a service station just outside Dorchester. My brother went to fill up the car with petrol. I left my father in the cafe whilst I went to the toilet. I stared in the mirror for a minute, looking at a wrinkle line that was beginning to take hold around the side of my mouth, and then popped a pill out of its foil strip and swallowed it with a gulp of water from the tap. When I got back to the cafe my father was sitting at a table with three drinks lined up in front of him. I raised my eyebrows. "Tea because I always have tea. Tango because I like Tango. And a smoothie because I've never had one before." He looked down at a map on the table in front of him and then took a long sip of the Tango. "What do you think about a little diversion?"

It took another hour to get to Studland Bay and when we pulled up behind the dunes my father got out of the car and began to undress. "Oh Jesus," said my brother. For a moment it looked as if he was taking everything off but when he got down to his pants he threw the rest of the clothes in the car and set off towards the water. All the hair on his body was snowy white and I noticed the considerable weight he – always a lean man – had put on whilst he had been ill. My brother and I climbed to the top of the dunes and watched him wade purposefully into the sea. It was beginning to get dusky and the beach was empty but I wondered what any onlooker might have made of this man, this scene. When the water was up to his waist he raised his arms above his head, dived in and swam. He was a strong, graceful swimmer, I had forgotten that. "I don't know whether to laugh or cry," said my brother. We had not known what we would find when we went to pick him up – we had hoped for something, certainly – but this, this was strange.

Over the next few weeks my father called me several times a day, often late at night or early in the morning – it was clear he wasn't sleeping very much. He was always excited, desperate to tell me about something he had read or seen on television, some new piece of information that had struck him forcefully, or report what he had been up to. He had been spending a lot of time in the woods that backed onto his house, looking out for bats and owls, sometimes sleeping out overnight so that he could be woken by the dawn chorus. He had started to build a treehouse in the back garden for my son and my brother's children, although this had got him into a row with the neighbours because of its size and the way it hung over their own garden ("fuck 'em," he said). He had joined an amateur dramatics society, and written "twenty or thirty" letters to the council and the local paper about a range of issues, none of which had yet been replied to or published. He had taken in a retired greyhound that he had seen pictured in a newsagent's window.

A month after we picked him up from Dorset, perhaps with memories of that expedition still fresh in his mind, he called to suggest we take a trip to the First World War battlefields and cemeteries in northern France. His own father had fought at the Somme and the Battle of Amiens and in the past, before he had been ill, we had sometimes talked of exactly this, a kind of pilgrimage. He had already spoken to my brother who had pleaded work and family commitments, no doubt truthfully.

"Given your situation," he said to me, "I imagine you are more flexible."

"What does Diane think about this?" I said.

"Well, your stepmother has moved out – temporarily."

Before I could gather a response he went on.

"I said a few things that upset her. Look, it's nothing to worry about. What about this trip? We'll eat steak frites, drink pastis, that sort of thing."

The fact was I could think of no compelling reason why I could not go. My situation, as my father called it, was that my four-year-old son lived with his mother, my ex-partner Helen, and her new boyfriend at the other end of the country, and my work came in fits and starts. It felt melancholy to be so available but the alternative, not going, staying at home, was barely more appealing.

"There isn't anywhere else you'd rather go? It's not all that uplifting a destination." "But it is, it is," he said with emphasis, "that's exactly what it is."

My father insisted on taking the overnight ferry from Portsmouth to St Malo, although this was not in any way a direct route. He said there was a romance to getting a cabin and sleeping on a boat, the sense of travel as a true experience. From there we would drive to Paris, spend the night, and then move on to the battlefields and cemeteries.

By the time we boarded the ferry there was only time to have a quick meal, watch the lights of the shore recede from the deck and then find the way to our cabin. It was the first of several nights sharing a room with my father and I do not think we had ever done it before as adults. His personal, intimate habits – the way he took his socks off last when he undressed and then put them on first in the morning, the rather horrible way he spat after cleaning his teeth – made him seem alien, unknown to me. My own rituals, unexposed now for some time, suddenly seemed old-mannish, even shameful – the plastic guard I wore to stop my teeth grinding and which left a bloody taste in my mouth in the morning, the earplugs, the pill I took discreetly in the tiny bathroom to help me sleep. My father gave no sign of being similarly discomfited. He was still awake reading a newspaper when I turned out the light above my bed. When the ferry P.A. system woke me in the morning to announce that we had docked, he was standing between the beds performing Tai Chi exercises.

It was clear that, since Dorset, my father had calmed down considerably. Even in his more manic moods, the chatter was not so continuous, so rambling, although his preoccupations were often no less surprising. These highs were also now interspersed with quieter more brooding periods, as if some of his intensity had turned inward. One of these moods seemed to descend on him as we drove out of St Malo, as it had the previous day on the way to Portsmouth. It was as if movement, the road, brought it on. He stared out of the window, at times fidgeting with the map that lay on his knees, perhaps lost in contemplation of the trip ahead and whatever it meant to him.

Ten kilometres or so beyond Rennes he turned away from the window and asked me what I wanted done with my body after my death. Whether this question had just occurred to him or was indicative of the general drift of his thoughts, I couldn't say. He did not wait for me to reply. "The Tibetans have a tradition of sky burial," he said. "I've been researching it – online. Incredible resource…" For a moment he seemed to have lost his thread, and I pictured his mind floating off to the far reaches of cyberspace. "The body is cut up and placed around the mountain top and vultures and other birds of prey eat the flesh. They believe that the spirit leaves the body in death, so there's no need to preserve it. There are practical reasons too, but it's also an act of generosity, giving yourself to other animals to sustain them. There are places you can do it here now – in Europe, I mean. There's something rather beautiful in the idea, don't you think? I'd much rather that than be turned to dust or left to rot in a grave."

"I've always rather liked the idea of a Viking burial," I said, "sent off in a burning ship, sword laid at my side, et cetera et cetera." I said this a little flippantly, an attempt to engage with my father's preoccupations, but I was struck, quite abruptly, by an image of myself – stretched out in a long boat, eyes closed, a faint smile on my lips but apparently dead, the skin of my hands and feet beginning to blacken and catch fire.

"Do you actually care what happens to you?" my father said, rather irritably.

"When I'm dead, I'm dead," I said. "I suppose I'm a materialist about these things. For me, the spirit dies too, whatever that is."

"I'll tell you a story," he said. "Twenty years ago scientists carried out an experiment where they killed a dog – killed it humanely – drained its blood and replaced it with some kind of preserving solution. Three hours later they put the blood back in and brought the dog back to life. Only problem was – the animal was completely mad, psychotic. Every time they tried it, the same result. They had to put all the dogs down."

I did not know what conclusions I was supposed to draw from this. When he did not continue I looked over at him.

"Hmmm…" he said vaguely, and then turned his attention back to the window.

We stopped for lunch in a village just beyond Laval. We sat outside in the pleasantly shady medieval square, and it was possible to feel like we were on holiday. My father seemed to have relaxed and was talking about his own father, stories I had heard many times before but was happy to hear again. Before the war my grandfather had worked on the trams in Blackpool and then for a chain of local cinemas. The cinemas all showed the same films but there was only ever one print so he cycled between them with the reels in the basket on the front of his bike, delivering and collecting them in a constant rotation to keep the films playing. When he went to enlist in 1914 he told them how old he was, sixteen, and the recruitment sergeant suggested he walk up and down the street and come in and tell them again. A picture of him taken before he went had always hung in my father's house, a formal shot, standing feet apart with some kind of cane braced between his hands, heartbreakingly young in his uniform. He had made a friend in France, Stan Cope, another sixteen-year-old, from South Wales, who was killed two months before the end of the war. We were going to visit Stan's grave in Amiens.

When we got back to the car my father asked to drive. He had not driven throughout his illness or since, as far as I knew.

"You can't do it all on your own," he said, and held out his hand for the keys.

At the slip road to the motorway, two hitchhikers were standing on the hard shoulder with their thumbs out.

"No one picks up hitchers anymore, Dad," I said, but he was already slowing down.

My father interrogated them as he drove, switching his attention between the backseat and the road ahead in a way that did not strike me as entirely safe. They were Bernard and Patti, a young Dutch couple on their way to Paris to stay with friends. Bernard had a shaven head, a ring through his lip and orange and red flames tattoed the length of his forearms. She was very pale-skinned, with short, bleached white hair and bright blue eyes. They were students in Amsterdam, both twenty-two years old, and had spent the summer travelling around France. Bernard was writing a thesis on prehistoric cave painting and they had been visiting important sites up and down the country. Bernard was forthcoming on all of this, eager to talk in his perfect, almost accentless English. Patti sat silently, smiling slightly and benignly, sometimes with her eyes closed.

"What's the story with those tattoos?" my father asked Bernard.

Bernard shrugged. "No story. A friend of mine did them. I thought they'd look good. You like them." It was a statement rather than a question.

"Not worried you might regret them when you're older," my father said, "my age perhaps? Or even my son's?" He indicated me with a thumb.

"I don't want to be the sort of person who has regrets." He was a little annoyed by the question, or pretending to be.

"Good answer," said my father thoughtfully, "good answer."

There was silence for several minutes and then my father said: "There's nothing more beautiful than a pregnant woman, right Bernard!"

Bernard laughed. I looked around at Patti. I had not noticed the way her dress tightened around the swell of her belly. She had her palms placed on either side of it, instinctively or absent-mindedly, the way pregnant women often do, as Helen had done when she was pregnant with our son. Patti saw me looking at her, and her smile widened.

I closed my eyes and pretended to be asleep as the conversation went on between my father and Bernard. My father began to philosophise about the raising of children. He felt – I had never heard him express views on this or seen evidence of it before – that modern parenting was so neurotic and controlling that it had created a world for children that was utterly dry, sterile and conformist. Children needed to experience fear, take risks, be free. "I have seen it with my own grandchildren," he said. I flicked my eyes open at this but then closed them again without speaking. Bernard agreed with him. He talked about his and Patti's plans for their child, from the home birth to the long trips they would take whilst it was still small, the virtues of openness, innocence and courage that they wanted to instil. My father described an old tradition that had been revived in Russia of baptising young children by dipping them in holes cut through frozen rivers and lakes. "Some say it erases sin," my father said. "The more prosaic view is that it's good for the immune system – and vitality in general. A little extreme, I'll admit." I had read about this too – some children

were said to have died this way. "Perhaps a little," Bernard said
tolerantly. "Right," my father went on, "but my point is…"

I pretended to be asleep, and then I was asleep.

When I woke up I could not tell how much time had passed.
My father was still talking.

"It's life and death, you know, two sides of the same coin,
the yin and the yang et cetera et cetera. In some ways, after all
that, I don't give a fuck. But in other ways I do, I absolutely do.
It gives you a different perspective, that's all."

In the mirror I could see Bernard nodding soberly,
apparently absorbing what my father had been saying. I
wondered what I had missed, what essential conversation this
might be the conclusion to. Regardless, my father seemed
satisfied that he had expressed himself as fully as was possible.
We were approaching Paris and for the rest of the journey, until
we dropped Bernard and Patti off at a station on the outskirts
of the city, no one spoke. My father gave Bernard his email
and phone number and insisted that they come and stay with
him when the child was born. Bernard tried to give my father
money for petrol but he refused. He hugged them both and I
awkwardly did the same.

"Nice kids," he said when we were back in the car.
"Stunning girl."

"Yes," I said.

My father had booked us into a faded and pretentious tourist hotel in the Latin Quarter. There was a liveried porter on the door, embossed stationery and a small, grimy window in our room that looked out over the domes of the Pantheon, which no doubt accounted for the excessive cost. The room was poky and full of odd angles, evidently subdivided from a more generous space. Crammed into it was a double bed with an ornate headboard, instead of the two singles my father had reserved.

I ran a hot bath and lay in it, staring at the ceiling. Through the wall, I could hear my father on the phone, with long pauses whilst the person on the other end of the line spoke. I could not make out what he was saying but the tone became steadily more irritable and then there was a somehow deeper silence and I knew that my father had hung up. He began whistling, always one of his habits. I lay there for another ten minutes whilst the water cooled and then got out.

Back in the bedroom, he was standing looking out of the window, still whistling.

"Diane says hello," he said, without turning around.

"Everything ok?"

"Oh, fine, fine. It's cold there apparently, raining."

"Right," I said.

"You know the history of the place?" He meant the Pantheon. "Louis XIV – or maybe it was Louis XV.... Anyway, he was dying of a mysterious fever and in his prayers he promised to build a church to Saint Genevieve if she cured him. The fever passed and this is what he built. Not the most beautiful building, but it has a certain grandeur I think. Later on, after the revolution, they turned it into a mausoleum – Victor Hugo, Voltaire, Rousseau, those guys."

"I didn't know that," I said.

He turned around and grinned.

"So now you do."

He went into the bathroom to wash and I called my son to wish him goodnight. I tried to do this every night, even though Helen had let me know that it was an inconvenience for her and perhaps not much fun for me or him either. Then I called my brother to let him know we were still in one piece. He laughed sympathetically and told me to keep him updated. "Rather you than me," he said.

"Cometh the hour, cometh the man," I said.

The evening was still warm and we had dinner sitting outside at the restaurant next to the hotel. We had steak which came very bloody and my father ordered a fifty euro bottle of red wine, even though I said I wasn't drinking. His mood had turned fidgety, distracted, and he barely ate. A small, mangy dog sat pleadingly near our table and he cut off strips of his meat and threw it on the ground.

My father started to talk about Stan Cope. Two days after the end of the Battle of Amiens, in August 1918, the beginning of the end of the war, Stan collapsed with a brain aneurysm. I had never heard this before, or had forgotten it – I had assumed he had been killed in the battle. "He was sharing a cigarette with my dad and just keeled over. He might have got a knock on the head but it could have happened to him anyway, war or no war. Strange way to go. Still, they buried him with the war dead – as they should."

My grandfather was twenty when he got back from the war. He married soon after, had six children, of whom my father was the youngest, and lived for another 75 years. He spoke freely about his years in France, and did not seem traumatised by it, although he used to say that he had seen enough of the rest of the world for one lifetime and never went further than Manchester again.

"Do you think they'll get married?"

My father had changed the subject.

"Who?"

"Helen and Jim." Jim was my ex's new boyfriend.

"I haven't the faintest idea."

"Do you think perhaps you should take an interest? Might have implications for you."

"You're a bit late with the paternal advice, Dad."

"I'm just concerned at how you've handled all this. As a child, you know – you were always rather fearful."

For all his talk over the last weeks, my father had not spoken to me about his illness, treatment or recovery, if that was what it was. I sensed some kind of taboo around it – his or my own, I couldn't say – as if to confront it directly might break whatever spell had been cast. The subject struck me as exhausting, irrelevant and dangerous all at the same time. But I felt moved to broach it now, when abruptly the waiter arrived to take our plates away.

My father ordered a coffee and by the time the waiter left the moment seemed to have passed. I went inside to use the toilet. There was a queue and when I came out my father was not at our table. I thought perhaps he had gone up to our room in the hotel to get something. The waiter brought his coffee but he still did not appear. Someone across the square shouted and I looked across to the giant-columned portico of the Pantheon. The two columns furthest to the right were covered in scaffolding – presumably to allow cleaning or restoration work to the frieze that lay across the width of the portico – and three quarters of the way up, perhaps 100 feet off the ground and climbing, was my father.

It took me a few moments to absorb this and by the time I had stood up and run over, passersby were already beginning to gather at the foot of the building to watch. The base of the scaffolding was boarded up but on one side an access door was open. Either my father had spotted this from the restaurant or he had just got lucky. Now he was scaling the ladders at speed and in very bad light. The crowd continued to gather. People called to him to come down. My father carried on, apparently oblivious, intent on whatever mission he had set himself. Something stopped me from calling out to him myself, shock perhaps, a reluctance to identify or associate myself with him, the knowledge that even if he heard me amongst the other voices it would likely make no difference.

When he reached the top level, he walked to the left-hand end of the scaffolding and climbed on to the narrow ledge underneath the frieze so that his back was pressed against the figures. He began to make his way slowly along the ledge. Someone shouted, "Don't do it" in French and someone else laughed. He stumbled slightly, steadied himself. He looked around and then down. He was a long way up, tiny against the looming mass of the church, but I was sure he was smiling. He held out his phone and seemed to take a photo – of the view or of himself, I couldn't tell.

It seemed to take forever for him to get down – I counted eleven ladders. Halfway down the final one he missed his footing and fell the few feet to the ground. The police and an ambulance had arrived and the crowd were pushed back and told to move on. I identified myself and was let through. My father was shaking, elated. Two policemen were asking him questions and a paramedic was holding his arm.

"Cold up there," he said to me.

"I can imagine," I said, but that was all I could say. I felt my legs begin to buckle and I sat down on the ground next to him, utterly drained.

We got back to the hotel at 3 a.m. and I took a pill to knock me out. At the police station my father had given a statement in which he offered no explanation for his stunt except that he was a little drunk and happy to be in Paris.
He was given a warning and told repeatedly that what he had done was very dangerous for him and for others, but the two officers seemed to feel they were dealing with a classic English eccentric rather than a criminal or a lunatic. They shook hands with both of us and wished us a good trip. At the hospital an x-ray of his right arm showed a small fracture and a nurse put it up in a sling.

I slept lightly, despite the pill, and from time to time, through my grogginess, I was aware of my father sitting in the chair by the window or moving around the room. When I woke up, around ten, I was lying diagonally across the bed and there was no sign of him, but I did not seem to have any worry left in me. I had a shower and went downstairs to have breakfast. He came in just as my food arrived, his arm strapped, his hair wild, and still wearing the clothes from the night before.

He sat down and poured himself some orange juice with his good arm.

"Beautiful day," he said.

He hadn't been able to sleep so had sat up reading before going out to find an early coffee and watch the sun come up. When the Pantheon had opened at nine he had gone down into the crypt to look at the tombs. He showed me a small lead model of the church that he had bought himself from the gift shop and then handed over a t-shirt that had a picture of the Eiffel Tower and above it the words "J'adore Paris".

"A memento of our trip," he said, almost sheepishly.

"You crazy bastard," I said.

"Perhaps don't tell your stepmother. And not so much of the old."

He finished his coffee and stood up.

"We should get going. It's blue skies out there."

He went upstairs to pack.

It was around three hours driving to Amiens, where my grandfather and Stan Cope had fought, and the cemetery where Stan was buried. After lunch we would go to the Somme Battlefields. We had a hotel booked in Arras for the night.

My father was quiet again. Once we had navigated our way out of Paris we didn't speak, but the silence felt companionable. About 50 kilometres from Amiens we crested a hill and suddenly we were amongst field after field of sunflowers. From there the land flattened out into the plains of the Somme valley and it was not hard to imagine vast armies inching backwards and forwards across the land. Soon we began to see the signs for the battlefields and cemeteries. We stopped at one of the roadside flower sellers and my father bought a bunch of red and yellow tulips.

St Pierre cemetery was a modest sized, unspectacular place, in a nondescript suburb of Amiens, backed on three sides by uniformly spaced yew trees. We walked through the iron entrance gates and past the stone of remembrance, engraved *Their Name Liveth for Evermore.* The sun was very bright and the clean white Portland stone of the headstones stood out like teeth against the immaculate green lawns. My father had brought a map and we found Stan's grave easily, half-way along the final row. Below the cross, it read *Private S Cope, The Queens, 28th August 1918, Age 19.*

My father laid the tulips next to the headstone and began to pick fussily at the neatly mown grass around it, as if determined to find weeds. I wandered along the row – some of the dead were younger than Stan – and was startled by the sound of my father's voice. At first I did not know who he was addressing, but then I recognised the poem. I did not know that my father read poetry, let alone knew any by heart. Perhaps he had learnt it at school, as I had. Standing in front of Stan's grave, his eyes closed, his bad arm hanging across his chest, again he seemed unfamiliar to me and somehow, briefly – I can think of no other word – heroic.

What passing-bells for these who die as cattle?
Only the monstrous anger of the guns.
Only the stuttering rifles' rapid rattle
Can patter out their hasty orisons.
No mockeries now for them; no prayers nor bells;
Nor any voice of mourning save the choirs, –

His voice began to crack but he kept going, with some effort. When he got to the end he sat down on the grass, buried his head in the crook of his fractured arm and began properly to cry. It began as a steady sob, moving on to a wail and then a kind of keening of pure, uninhibited sorrow. Whatever brittle barrier had penned this in over the last weeks had broken, it seemed to me, and out it came, torrentially, ecstatically.

I did not know whether to try and stop him or at least move him along, out of the cemetery and back to the car, somewhere more discreet, although we seemed beyond that now. There were a few other people walking amongst the graves but we did not seem to have attracted anyone's attention. Perhaps it was unremarkable in a place like this. I hesitated to intervene with him, such was the elemental force of his emotion. He did not seem to be trying to stop. Then I sat down too and put my arm around him, and he wept into my chest.

His face was red and swollen and his eyes bloodshot but by the time we drove out of the car park my father had recovered his composure. We had planned to go on another hour or so and find somewhere for lunch, but as soon as we crossed a bridge over the Somme river – I had not realised that it was this that gave the area and the battle its name – he asked me to pull over.

On both sides the road was lined with fields of corn, six to eight feet high. My father got out of the car and, after walking up and down for a minute, disappeared into it. For perhaps two minutes I sat in the car, the engine still on. I took the strip of pills out of my wallet and swallowed two with a gulp of the flat Diet Coke that my father had been drinking the day before. Then I pulled the car further off the road, got out and locked it. In among the corn there was the sound of water. The stalks were bent and trampled where my father had passed through. I went on for several minutes to where the field gave way to a small pebbly beach on the river bank. The river was narrow here, perhaps 15 metres wide, and ran quickly. There were willows trailing their branches in the water on the opposite side. My father's clothes and the sling for his arm lay on the beach.

I shaded my arms against the sun and spotted him, out in the river, a little downstream. His arms were in the air and at first I thought he was struggling in the current, but then I saw he was gesturing for me to come in. I began to undress, laying my clothes next to my father's. The skin of my ankles prickled as it touched the water and I thought for a second of children dipped in freezing lakes and rivers. I thought of the places we were yet to visit, the strange resonance of their names – Thiepval, Ypres, Passchendaele. I thought I felt the familiar, peaceful flood of the pills begin to wash over me, but it was too soon for that. I went on into the current.

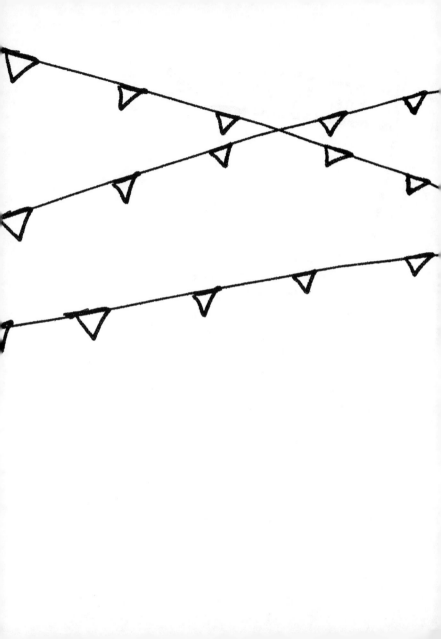

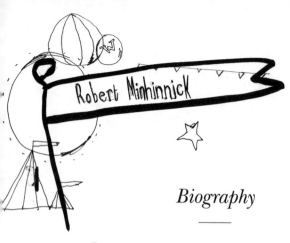

Biography

ROBERT MINHINNICK is a Welsh novelist
and poet whose works include *Sea Holly*
(Seren), *King Driftwood* (Carcanet),
*Fairground Music: The World of Porthcawl
Funfair* (Gomer) and most recently *The Keys
of Babylon* (Seren). His book *New Selected
Poems* (Carcanet) is due out this year. Robert
won the Forward Prize for best individual
poem in 1999 and 2003, Wales Book of the
Year in 1993 and 2006 and was shortlisted
for the Ondaatje Prize in 2008. He works
in the environmental movement, having
co-founded Friends of the Earth Cymru in
1984 and Sustainable Wales in 1997. He is
married with one daughter.

El Aziz: Some Pages from His Notebooks

by

Robert Minhinnick

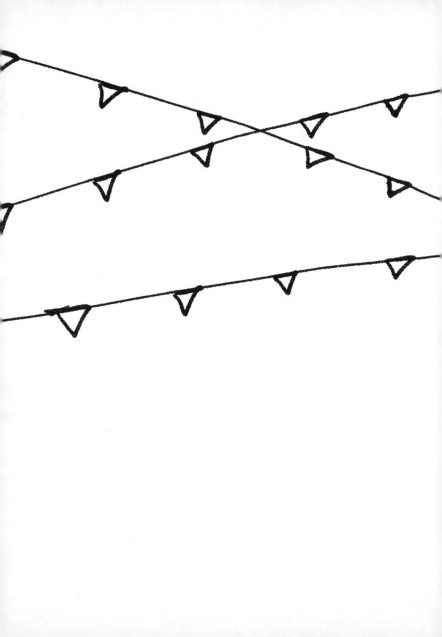

Even for that season it was hot. I went west along the coast and found myself in Nerja, everything shivering like cellophane in the haze.

I saw they had built a palace where the dunes had been. Once the dune pools held egrets. They had reminded me of home. Creeping close I could glimpse the birds' reflections in the water. Now there were fountains, but the fountains were turned off, and the swimming pools empty. After the first palace was a castle. After that castle another castle. Or palace. Each castle was fifty apartments piled on top of one another. Towers and minarets, but all empty. No cars in the parking places and the dune grass like wire breaking through the tar. And everywhere the signs; some Se Vende, some For Sale. But the English have stopped coming. Suddenly there are no English.

At last I saw a man and I asked him about a job. A watchman's job. A caretaker.

I'm going to Madrid, he said. My cousin has a tapas bar. The polytunnels are for the Africans.

I was in Madrid once and saw the living statues in Plaza Mayor. It crossed my mind. Who would I be? I thought of Picasso. They named the airport in Malaga after him. Then I thought of Lorca. I saw a plaque for him in Benal Madena. I looked up from the street and there it was. But how does a poet dress?

Then I thought of Clint Eastwood, the man with no name,
the thin cigarillo between thin lips. Who would dare refuse him
money? A fistful of dollars? But I would have to stand on a box.

No men are tall where I come from. Even in this place, they
call me Lazarillo. The little Lazarus.

I turned a corner and war had been declared. There were the
Rangers supporters and there were the police. Grown men
were vomiting in the street. There were police horses with white
eyes, men with helmets and shields. The warriors are called The
Gers, a Glaswegian tribe half-naked and painted blue, singing
outside GMex and The Thistle. I trod the broken glass around
the Briton's Protection Hotel. A gallon of Grunt, an eight pack
of indigo SuperT. Bellies brimming with gold. I thought of
the desert I had once crossed – all that ash as if the world had
burned. Goat herders in their cinder-coloured rags.

I used to sell the *Big Issue* near Woolworths. I used to tell the
people who I was and that I had come here for a better life.
Across the road, outside Streets nightclub, a woman older than
my mother would play the accordion, its white teeth brown as
nicotine. She knew only one tune. Then Woolworths closed.
Then the nightclub closed. Some boys took her accordion and
stepped on it. How it groaned in terror. I heard its protest and

went to help. The boys were gone and I was glad. Those boys in their hoods, their trackwear, glancing at their screens.

Today I have been cutting cloth. When he gave me the job, the man didn't ask my name. The bale of silk was cold as river water in my hands and upon my chest. We might have been anywhere. But there was a newspaper, the *Manchester Evening News*, and packets of teabags. After a few days I knew where I was. We were working in a warehouse on an estate off the Salford Road. There were two English women who smoked when the bosses weren't looking. One burned a hole in the fabric and they had to hide it.

There are no windows in our building, and the strip light hums. Our toilet is at the end of the corridor. How the women sigh when they see it. They bring their own soap, their own paper, and there is a bootmark on the door.

Have a break, the man said yesterday. We were all surprised, but we couldn't go anywhere. There is a yard with puddles and piebald ice, and the German shepherd on a chain keeps the people out, keeps the people in.

When I woke this morning it was dark, darker even than the Euphrates where I once rolled at night in its velvet bed.
I found the costume outside the Piccadilly hotel. Somebody had been sick on it but I sponged it down with hot water and Lenor in the laundry room.

This evening I walked into the Woodlands lounge. There were a good group of the residents there. Two or three saw me at once, then all turned their heads. The men cheered. Then everyone clapped. It was December 28 and I was Santa Claus, a green Santa Claus in a green Santa costume, a green Santa hat. Only the boots were missing. I have a pair of trainers from the sale they have at St Michael's every Saturday. My other shoes have come to pieces.

Bit late aren't you, Laz? called one of the men. Or do your lot have Christmas on a different date?

My room at Woodlands is small and next to the boiler. Sometimes I hear the pipes grumbling, like an accordion. The manager said it's not ideal but she needs people to stay overnight.

I understand that. Night nurses are expensive. Roisin said they used to have schoolgirls and they slept in the lounge. But they were bad. They were wicked girls. They took the box of Yellowtail wine from the cupboard and lay on the floor and drank from its tap.

Now they have me. At night I walk the corridors. I stand in the kitchen reading the rotas, the tickets on the fire extinguishers. I open the freezers and their doors rise with a sigh and the cold smokes. And there is tomorrow, foretold within the freezers. There are our burgers, our frozen fairycakes. There are all tomorrow's parties. All in their icy envelopes, an industrial ice the colour of old women's skin.

I look around the kitchen. How still it is. Like a photograph of itself, I think.

There is a cockroach on the floor. I listen to the sound it makes, an electrical sound, a tickering of a watch. I once shared a room up a flight of steps in Malaga. We were watching television in the afternoon and I had poured orange juice. When I picked up the plastic cup there was a cockroach in it. We all gathered round to watch it swim. All seven of us, making bets on whether cockroaches drown.

There are only mugs here so I make a mug of tea and take it to the lounge. Three a.m. I put the television on, very low, and flick through the seventy-two channels. There are always more channels now. Like books and magazines. Like cockroaches. Sometimes I play the DVDs the residents' families bring. I have watched *Titanic* and listened to the real ice rise in its cliffs, its cordilleras. I have watched *Descent* and seen the women lost in the dark caves.

What a strange film, I think, to bring your mother, your grandmother. Women lost in the dark, their torches dimming, almost out. And I have settled back and listened to the silence.

At 4 a.m. there was a good show. The British are pure, it said. Eighty per cent of the British have common DNA. It can be traced back 12,000 years to hunters who followed the reindeer to Britain. Not so many, those hunters. A few hundred. There was a picture of people in skins, children wrapped in furs. They trudged the frosty ground, past stunted trees. Then on the news there were more demonstrations. British jobs for British workers, the banners said. Yes, I said. Yes I understand.

But do they understand, I wonder, the old people here? Understand that it's only me tonight? The manager away, Roisin away, everyone else away. Only me on duty tonight, only me in my green Santa suit.

I. Me. Their only guard. Me in the silence. Not even a clock tickering. All the clocks digital here, and all around me the Christmas food. Boxes of liqueurs, mince pies in biscuit tins. And chocolate money in gold, in silver foil.

I collect the chocolate money and look at it. My treasure. These coins I can see in the dark, a glint from the coins, a glimmering. Maud who knits, Magdalena who knits, gone to their beds whilst here in the darkness are their fortunes abandoned. String bags of coins as a miser would hoard. A miser from the fairytales.

Those tales make misers miserable but I have always believed misers the happiest of people. It's not what money

might buy that makes the misers happy. No, it is the metal of
the money itself. Its chinking coin, its smell of other hands, its
coolness on the skin. And such a pillow those coins make. For
the head or for the heart.

I bite into a chocolate liqueur. Its dark green taste is a
mouthful of the night river. I steal the chocolate, I who was
once the night swimmer, I who kept the key to the city of
Babylon on a cord around my neck.

I had seen Woodlands when delivering leaflets in Slaughter
Street. The Alpha Interiors leaflet was orange and said all blinds
were 10 per cent off, plus free home consultation. The leather
sofa people were offering 50 per cent off the Relaxo Recliner,
and more for the Ritzy. Happy Dreamz was half price too, all
their beds unbeatable bargains.

I remember that often in Babylon Aadam's car wouldn't
start, which meant we couldn't get home to sleep. Business
was always bad in Babylon when I was there. Not that I stayed
long. There were only Russian tourists then, and few of them.
Sometimes a bus would come with retired doctors and teachers
from the city. But it was usually quiet. Aadam sat and smoked
like a grand vizier while I took the entrance money, sold
postcards and maps, water and dates. When his Nissan couldn't
go we would lock the gate and wander around.

I sat with him once in the Street of Processions, the car pushed under the wall, and listened to his stories. Aadam, with his yellow skin, his camphorated clothes, knew all of our history. His father or his grandfather had fought the English in the 1930s. Now there are jobs in the English graveyard, he told me. Cutting grass, keeping the children out. Steady work. Above our heads, carved in the stone, I knew there were creatures not from this world.

One night we sat in the weeds beside the black lion. The masters of stone had carved the lion devouring a foreigner, some enemy of our city.

Look, said Aadam, pointing up. That is Mars.

The planet was bright as a spark from his cigarette. Then Aadam asked me what I would do. Where I would go.

A friend is in Spain, I said. Good prospects.

It was so hot that sleeping out was no problem. Sometimes I eased myself into the river and allowed my body to be wrapped in its green sheets. And many times I lay under the palms and listened to that river sliding by. Slow as blood. I could hear its echo in the ground, the current breathing in my ear.

I also heard another sound. Two lovers crept into the grove. They paused and whispered, embraced and lay down, whispered and laughed. Then went their way. I could see the stars through the trees. Silverfish, I thought, on mother's pantry stone. Mars was lower now and red as myrrh. It seemed to be coming nearer.

No one in Slaughter Street would ever buy a new leather sofa. I could have told them that. But I delivered the leaflets anyway. When I came back I sat on the wall of the Mount Joy Club. Tanya would be singing there next Tuesday, followed by karaoke. I watched the taxis pass. Every one was driven by a Pakistani. In town, the people selling the *Big Issue* were now Romanians. I sometimes see them go behind Boots and speak on their mobile phones. A beautiful language, I have come to think. But all the morning I looked at Woodlands.

One day I remember I call the good day. I turned down Evening Street, which was a redbrick terraced street. Once I had delivered leaflets here. Now it was morning and people had gone to work. There was a milk carton on the step of the first house. I took it. Halfway down Evening Street was a packet of two Sheldon soft white batons on a doorstep. I took it. At the end of Evening Street was a wall with a bramble growing over it. Snagged on the thorns was the green string of a purple balloon. Attached to the string was a card from the Salvation Army. I read the card. It said come to our hostel. Our army hostel.

Two streets later was a park behind railings. I sat on a bench
there and ate the bread and drank the milk. The bread stuck
to the roof of my mouth in a paste but I finished every crumb.
I watched a woman put a Tesco plastic bag over her hand
and pick up her dog's shit. She placed the shit and the bag in
another Tesco plastic bag and tied the bag's mouth. The woman
looked at me. Then she spoke to her dog.

On the next bench was a postman. He was wearing blue
shorts and had orange flashes on his pouch. I looked at his
pouch and it was bursting with envelopes. Every pocket in that
pouch bursting with envelopes. What a good man, I thought.
Such a solemn duty. Delivering letters to the world. The world's
news. Like me, he was drinking from a milk carton. Cheers
mate, he said.

Bins and beds, the woman in Woodlands had said. That's easy to
remember, isn't it?

Yes it is, I thought, because I am a quick learner. Bins and
beds. I take the black plastic bags that the residents leave in a
place they call the scullery and put them in the wheelies outside.
The wheelies are emptied on Monday and Thursday mornings.

There are forty residents, and I thought that would mean
many bags. But these old people don't waste much. They are
careful people, they have always been frugal.

The beds are stripped every week, the sheets, the duvet covers, the pillow cases. We also have the residents' clothes for their weekly wash. Mostly, their strange underwear.

How we laugh, Roisin and I, at the underwear of every Lady Ga Ga. Zhao Si never laughs because he is a real launderer. How sad it is, that underwear. Revealing their last secrets. The last secrets of their lives. When Roisin says 'gussets' we know when to laugh. It is our codeword. A detonator.

And it will never end. When someone leaves, a room is not long empty. Another woman arrives, frail, tearful, making the best of it, her family around her, soon glad to get out. Up or down in the lift they go and out into the rain, across the road to the Mount Joy Club car park, over to Slaughter Street. Back in the rain to their Ford Fiestas, the husband and wife, the son or the daughter. Crying. Sighing with relief.

I opened the lounge door, closed it carefully, and crossed the grass. The wall is only one metre high and then I was on the petrol station forecourt. Then another wall, then the slip road and I was within the Tesco car park. Trains of trolleys in their bays, one car in all the frozen field, frost on its windscreen like a grey eggshell. An egret's dirty egg.

Inside I walk the aisles. Such a strange light. A dead light, I think, yet bright. Deathly bright. A camera follows me, then another, and a security man stands at the end of the aisle, watching, arms folded. Then he moves. But not far. I pass the avocados, I pass the butternut squash. Like bells, I think, the squash. I pass the toothpaste, I pass the place where people buy Caribbean holidays and insurance for their silver cars.

Tesco is open twenty-four again. Life is returning to normal. I put the chocolate money in my basket. They are half-price now, the golden coins. I go through the bin with its cut-price DVDs. Here is one, *Day of the Dead*. I put it in my basket. So many movies now about the dead, the dead people who cannot die.

Maud broke her hip today. She slipped and the ambulance took her away. We know she will not come back, that she has taken the last step but one. Maud's knitting is on her chair in the lounge but I am thinking instead about Roisin in the laundry, where she showed us her own underwear.

Enough of these, she laughed. These crappy keks. Cop this, Lazza.

And she unzipped her jeans and there was her red thong. Red fur within the squash. No, I thought. Cleft of a peach. An Andalusian peach. I stood in the street eating a peach, its juice dribbling on my chin and I looked up and saw Lorca's plaque. So many poets.

I used to stand under the statue of the poet outside
the Baghdad museum. At five, the girls would pass, in their
dark glasses, their red lipstick, hurrying from the Ministry of
Information.

Now that's what I call underwear, Roisin said. Even Zhao Si
laughed and leered, who never laughs but leers as a lizard will
in its cold blood. I remember the wall lizards at home. They
smiled like old men. Never trust the old men, my mother said.
Do not go with them.

At the checkout the man looked hard at me. Then smiled.

Bargains, he said. Lots of bargains now. Bit late for that,
isn't it? he asked, and brushed his fingers on the sleeve of my
green suit. A gentle touch, I thought. But a dismissal.

Outside, the Fiesta was still there. I tried to scrape the ice
on the driver's side but it was too thick. I wanted to look within,
I don't know why. Such a winter. I remember Malaga's yellow
steps, the peaches piled in pyramids on the market stalls.

It was 3 a.m. and I crossed the car park with my Tesco bag.
I pictured myself in the stony light of the camera screen.
When I paused the camera paused. When I passed the
camera followed.

Roisin has often asked how old I am. She knows I am older than I look.

We were in the Tesco cafe where we meet two other Iraqis. And the Albanian. We go there because Roisin says it is good to get out. To see friends. Roisin says she is going mad, surrounded by all the old women. All she can think of, she says, are the tea stains on their blouses, the old women's tights like seaweed flung over the Donegal rocks.

But the Tesco girls are kind to us. One teabag and one lemon slice costs me one pound sterling. But there are free refills.

We should plan a night out, Roisin says. Go across to the Mount Joy. The Albanian boy smiles and smiles. The Iraqi boys smile and smile. Everyone loves Roisin.

I think of the couple under the palm trees, lying upon the crackling fronds. Aadam once told me there were crocodiles in the river and not to swim there. He said it was in the Christian Bible, in the Book of Isaiah. All the children who went missing, Aadam insisted, were eaten by the crocodiles.

So I pointed towards the palace on its hill. To the ziggurat where we were never supposed to point. I said to Aadam, yes, of course. And is the great crocodile himself at home today? If so, from which of his six hundred rooms is the great crocodile spying on us?

Aadam laughed and rolled his eyes. Not so loud, he said. Not so loud.

That day in the Plaza Mayor, I had looked at the human statues. No, not a poet. No, not Clint Eastwood. Instead, a terrible thought had entered my head. I gasped at myself. I reeled at the impact of such a thought.

Why couldn't I be the crocodile? The crocodile dressed as some of the Bedouin still dress, in the black jalabiya of Badiet esh Sham. Those desert-coloured robes. Yes, I could be the crocodile. The crocodile with his fierce moustache. His hand held up in peace.

Hey Lazza, said Roisin, reaching out to touch me. It was as if she woke me from a dream. When are you going to tell us what door your key opens?

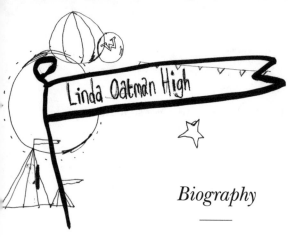

Linda Oatman High

Biography

LINDA OATMAN HIGH is an author, journalist, playwright, poet and screenwriter who is a lifelong resident of Lancaster County, Pennsylvania. She has published several stories and articles in the UK's *My Weekly* and *The Sunday Post*, and thousands in the US. Linda's books for children and teens have won many awards including the 1999 Top of the List Best Picture Book of the Year for her book *Barn Savers*. Linda holds an MFA in Writing from Vermont College, and graduated in 2010 at the age of 52. Her family includes her husband John – the Barn Saver – as well as four grown children and grandchildren.

Nickel Mines Hardware

by

Linda Oatman High

———

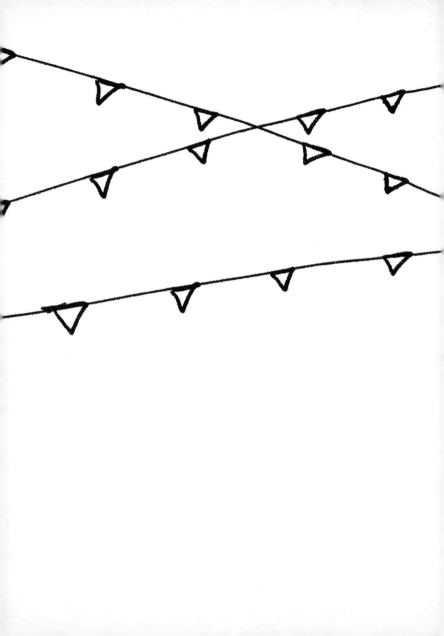

Flex ties, plastic, two bags. Eye bolts. Nails, tubes, clamps. These are the things he bought, right before he shot up the school and killed all those girls.

Katie Zook knew who he was: the milkman. Thin wispy hair the color of hay, ordinary wire-framed glasses. A tall and lean man, with a bit of a befuddled barn owl look about him.

She rang up his things on the cash register, 9:14 a.m. and again at 9:16, when he remembered something that he forgot. Eye bolts. He needed eye bolts, eye bolts, the strongest kind, where are they? His eyes were crazy, wild, like an animal that knows it is set for slaughter.

Katie tucked the receipt in the paper bag with his purchase, and she came from behind the counter. She wondered later why she didn't just stay where she was.

"Second aisle," she said. "On the left, just above your head."

She led the way, past the Radio Flyer wagon, the sleds, the tools. Past the plumbing fixtures and garden supplies and bird seed and kerosene lanterns, the farm toys and the carbide lamps.

He walked too close. His boots pounded, hammering hard on the warped wooden floorboards.

Katie stopped, pointed at the pegboard. A board creaked beneath her feet, a warning of something underneath not quite strong. The store dog – a rangy German Shepherd named Jake – growled from under the counter. *He* knew.

The milkman's breath was heavy, and there was the stale smell of coffee, of breakfast. Katie saw that his hand shook as he took a bag of eye bolts from a hook.

The best kind, $5.99. Katie sold these to people who wanted to hang paintings, big heavy paintings, so that they would not sway or fall. A sturdy string attached to an eye bolt attached to a nail on the wall. That made sense.

Katie was 18, and she still lived on the farm with her parents. Not married, not yet, she wanted to be a school teacher but ended up working here for now: a clerk at Nickel Mines Hardware. The store, built long before Katie was born, nestled snug into the corner of Vintage and Valley, just down the road from home.

Katie had worked here at the store since July, a long time. Corn had turned from tall leafy stalks hanging with green and gold to stubby brown, flowers died or went underground, and the view from the wavy-pane window of the hardware store was sparser now. More beige, more dry, spare and orderly beneath a bright cornflower sky. The skies of October always seemed to hold more blue. Maybe they knew that winter was coming, too. The autumn skies were stocking up, as Mother did with her jars of canned peaches and beans, trying to preserve and keep just a little taste of summer.

On that day of the beginning of the fall, Katie watched through the window as the milkman got in his truck, his dirt-brown pickup truck filled with weapons and boards and two bags from Nickel Mines Hardware, and he drove away. The milkman just drove away, down the road, past Katie's home. He drove to the school, and then it began.

The names of the girls bolted tight to Katie's brain. She couldn't stop thinking those names inside of her head, like a poem or a prayer she knew by heart: Naomi Rose. Marian. Anna Mae. Mary Liz and Lena, sisters. *Dead.* Five little girls dead; five others in hospital beds.

And the hand that held that gun, the hand that pulled that trigger, had touched Katie's hand when it shoved a ten-dollar bill across the counter, paying for the eye bolts.

"Keep the change," the milkman said.

There was no telephone in the hardware store, and so news sometimes came from the sky. The first sign was the whirring of helicopter wings. The front door was propped open with a brick, catching the fresh morning air so that it would circulate in the store.

Katie was re-arranging the pegboard, moving bags to different hooks. It felt a little bit like playing Checkers: the careful weighing of movements, the deliberation, the sense of purpose.

Katie picked up some bags that the milkman must have knocked off with his nervous hands, and she hung them up again, smoothly slipping hooks through holes in bags. Katie was good at her job, that much she would say, even if it sounded proud. Katie cared about keeping things neat, making each receipt a perfect little record of what the day had accomplished.

The choppy sound of the helicopter caught her attention. Katie dropped a tiny rattling bag of hardware, rounded a barrel of nails, headed for the door. The dog tagged along, ears at attention, paws padding and clicking upon the floor. Dust motes floated through slanting beams of light that cut through the stale mustiness of the inside of the store. Katie and Jake stepped outdoors, into fresh air, onto the wooden porch.

The helicopter slashed through the blue. The silver wings seemed to speak – *Hurry Emergency Hurry Emergency Hurry Emergency* – as they sliced the sky. The plane flew in the direction of her home, in the direction of the school. A light blinked off, on, off, on.

Katie shaded her eyes. She heard sirens, many sirens, screaming, wailing. Something was wrong, oh, my; so very wrong.

Katie had never heard so many sirens crying at one time. She bent down and retrieved the key, the hidden antique skeleton key, from under the mud-encrusted rag rug on the porch.

Katie locked the door. She started to walk away from the store. The dog followed, too close, snuffling, nose up.

Katie took a few steps, hesitated, and then went back and tested the door knob again.

It was locked.

Nickel Mines Hardware remained closed, closed for the day, closed for tomorrow, closed for the week. There were funerals to focus upon, caskets to make, white capes and burial dresses to sew. A cloak of mourning settled over the store, over the school, over the farms and the fields and the roads.

Katie attended. She attended each and every one: Naomi Rose. Marian. Anna Mae. Mary Liz and Lena. She felt so close to each one, and after all, she'd known them all as babies, as clumsy tots, as graceful girls growing tall and sweet as Silver Queen corn. Smart, too. The little girls were all so smart, quick as whips with intelligence, and with big hearts and kind souls to boot.

"Shoot me first." That's what the oldest one – Marian, who was 13 – said to the milkman. Her little sister Barbie said, "Shoot me second." Barbie survived, and she was the one who told the story, who told of how the milkman asked the class to pray for him.

"Those five little angels must have been very special, to have been chosen for this." That's what the bishop said, nodding his head and stroking his beard, his long gray beard.

There wasn't much space between Katie and those girls. All that came between them was the milkman, a mile of road and sky, and not very many minutes. Katie saw those wild crazy set-for-slaughter eyes and not much later the girls saw them, too. Those eyes and those hands tied them together: the little girls and Katie Zook. Katie wished she could have stopped him, could have kept the milkman at the store somehow. If only she had known what was to come. If only she had known.

Flex ties, plastic, two bags. Eye bolts. Nails, tubes, clamps. These are the things he bought. These are the things Katie sold.

Another Monday, just one week, hard to believe. It was time for Katie was go back to work. The funerals were finished, but people were still coming in herds to visit.

They and their cars invaded this place where the unthinkable had happened, as if they had to see in order to believe. People leaned from open car windows, requesting directions to the school in voices quivering with respect. Kindness softened their faces, but Katie still felt invaded.

Couldn't anything be private? Cameras like eyes were all over the place, recording, recording. Taking pictures to look at later. Katie guessed they never wanted to forget, but still. Who could ever forget this?

There had been three school shootings in the United States that week, last week. This was the Amish 9/11, the people said. We are flying our flags at half-mast, they said, for you. The whole world is watching, and we are learning. We are in awe of you. We are completely in awe. You are setting an example for all of us to follow. What grace, what faith!

They were brave, and they asked questions. The people were mostly curious about forgiveness, about how the Amish could forgive this. Katie had no answer for that.

Katie was still working on forgiveness. She had not attended the service for the milkman, but her family did. Her father offered a heartbreaking little bouquet of wildflowers, and her mother baked a pie, a shoo-fly, for the shooter's wife.

"Oh, it was the saddest thing I've ever seen," said Katie's mother after the milkman's funeral. "Over half of the crowd was Amish, and the wife fell to her knees with weeping. The milkman's father, the police officer, was beside himself with grief. Just beside himself, Katie. You should have come with us. It was really something to see."

Katie's father endlessly recited the verse of Matthew 6:14, from the King James Bible, and he said it in English and in Dutch, for double effect. He is dramatic, Katie's father. *"For if ye forgive men when they sin against you, your heavenly Father will also forgive you."*

Katie tried, oh, she tried with all her might. She attempted once again to read *The Martyr's Mirror*, as Mother suggested. But this dusty old book, ancient Dutch accounts of people joyfully waiting to die for their faith, was written in the 1600s. Katie feels much space between this and that.

The writers of that book knew nothing of *this*: a milkman who is a customer when Katie is just doing her job, a good job. A milkman who leaves a hardware store and drives to a schoolhouse on a normal Monday morning and shoots up all those girls. Boring old meticulously written accounts of those who suffered, were burned on stakes and locked in prisons, don't make *this* suffering any better.

The entire terrible *world* is a prison. That's what Katie knew.

Early morning, before dawn. Even the sun wasn't up yet. The moon wasn't quite sure what to do, although the stars were all gone. The sky streaked purple and pink, the color of cotton candy at the farmers fair. This was farm show season, a time that Katie usually loved. Not now. Cotton candy seemed too sweet for times like this, too fluffy, too full of spun sugar, light and air. So she would not go. No. It was time to get back to work, to move on, to go forth.

Katie rode her bicycle, pedals spinning round and round just like always, propelling her forward, just like it was any ordinary Monday morning.

She decided to take the long way around, and Katie made a quick and sudden turn to the left, the scary direction: White Oak Road, past the school.

Yellow police tape surrounded the school grounds, flapping, tattered. Three swings swayed empty, creaking in morning breeze. It was creepy, so queer to see those empty yet moving swings. Katie, tormented now with bad dreams, had the uneasy feeling of being inside of one of those dreams. Trapped within a nightmare, with no escape. This was the price she paid, for being here in this place, where maybe she was not supposed to be. But still. Katie just had to *see*.

Katie and each and every one of her brothers and sisters had all been students at this school. Jacob, Jonas, Lydia, Rachel, Emma, Levi, Eli, Sadie, closest in age to Katie. *Sadie.* Katie attempted not to think much about Sadie: the shunning, the excommunicating. Sadie was dead to them, that's what Father said. She was dead to them.

Sadie had been large with child, out of wedlock, a sin. The bishop declared Shunning, and so the family shunned. No speaking, no seeing, no eating together, no letters. It has been over a year: 368 days since Katie saw her last.

But she tried not to think about that.

The windows were boarded, but the school was unlocked. Katie discovered that when she stepped over the caution tape and walked cautiously to the door. It swung slowly open, a wary invitation to come inside.

The schoolroom was a mess: tipped desks, topsy-turvy. Windows were shot out; shattered glass crunched beneath Katie's feet. She stopped. *Oh. Oh, my word.* Bloodstains, splattered, on the floor, on the wall, under the chalkboard under the poster.

Visitors Brighten People's Days. That's what the poster said.

Katie was still shaking when she arrived at the store. The sun was up; the moon gone. Jake waited on the porch, tail swishing as if nothing was wrong.

Katie leaned her bicycle against the side of the building (she kept forgetting to get that silly kickstand fixed), and she went up the steps, retrieving the key and unlocking the door. Jake flopped down, a contented bag of bones, and he stayed lazily on the porch, head on paws, tail thumping. Jake was lucky to be a dog, to forget so soon, to find everything to be fine as long as he was lying in sunshine. What a simple and pure life, to be a dog in sunshine.

It smelled the same inside, the reassuring odor of kerosene and wood chips and new tools, mixed vaguely with the spicy aftershave of the non-Amish customers. It looked the same. Rows and rows of hardware, lined up like solid helpers for the jobs – the good and honorable jobs – that people needed to do.

Katie pushed the button that opened – *ding!* – the cash register. She counted the money, remembering not to lick her index finger in-between the bills. She pulled out the pad for receipts, and she stacked the brown paper bags. Katie knew what to do, and she went through all the motions of a normal morning at Nickel Mines Hardware.

A car pulled into the gravel parking lot, tires crunching through stone. Once again, Katie felt the crunch of broken glass beneath her feet back at the school. *No. She would not think about that again; she would not.*

Jake barked. The car was red, bright as blood. Katie watched through the cracked side window of the store, as the car parked in an automobile space beside the row of hitching posts. Nickel Mines Hardware was pleased to advertise that they made accommodations for both the English and the Amish, that they discriminated against none. Unless, of course, they were shunned.

It was a woman, a young lady with a curtain of hair the color of mum's: orange. She was a worldly woman, Katie could tell from in here. Painted face, lips stained red, flashy earrings dangling in big wire circles like surprised mouths hanging from her ears. A clown. The woman looked like a clown.

The woman leaned into the backseat, reached in, and lifted out a baby.

She hoisted the child to her shoulder and made her way to the porch. Katie moved to a different window, where she could see the pink button of the baby's face, nestled into the woman's shoulder. Katie loved babies; the newness of them, the perfect little innocence of a teeny-weeny being that did not yet know evil.

The woman stepped onto the porch and Katie could see the swishy broom of Jake's tail sweeping the air.

"Hey, Jakey," the woman said. Katie caught her breath. *Could it be ... ?*

It was. The woman with the long orange hair and the painted face and the pink-faced baby was Sadie, Katie's big sister, her sister that Katie had not seen for 368 days.

"I was hoping you'd be working," Sadie said. Her gaze, so familiar with green eyes the color of springtime grass, nailed itself to Katie's face. Katie felt the flush, spreading from her cheeks to her ears.

"How did you know that I work here?" Katie smoothed back her hair, even though not a strand had escaped from the tight bun stretched taut, gathered beneath the gauze of Katie's covering.

"Oh, I keep track," said Sadie. "Remember my best friend Emma from school?"

Katie nodded. "Emma S.," she said. "The one who loved to churn butter."

"Yes. Well, Emma never held to the Shunning. We keep in touch. She's even been to visit me in the city, in New York. She takes the train. I give her clothes to change when she gets there, and we go out on the town. She especially loves this space-theme place in Times Square: Mars 2112. They have great butter."

Sadie laughed, the same old ring of merriment like wind chimes.

"You live in the city? New York City?" Katie was incredulous. She has heard of the place, with its taxi cabs and buildings stretching to heaven and underworld trains to take people places. So strange.

Sadie nodded. She shifted the baby, rotating it so that the face turned to Katie.

"Meet Grace," she said. "She's three months next week."

Katie reached out, touched the baby's face, stroked her cheek. "She is so pretty. My niece. Hello, Grace."

"Would you like to hold her?"

Sadie held out the baby, an offering, and Katie took it. She took her.

"She smells nice," Katie said, nose buried in the baby's duck-fuzz head. The child felt good, so good – warm – in Katie's arms. Holding her, this pink-faced fragrant baby, Katie felt as if she held the world.

She held everything.

Sadie had not come to purchase anything. She had come to see Katie, just to see Katie, and to make sure that everybody else was well. She had driven for more than three hours, in that red car that she said she rented.

"I just could not believe it when I saw the news on TV," said Sadie. "I was in shock, and just started pacing the floor, walking in circles. It took a week for me to get my act together and get down here to see for myself."

"Did you go inside the school?" Katie asked. She still held the baby. Grace, her niece, sleeping now.

"No." Sadie shook her head, the curtain of mum-colored hair swinging over her face. Katie wondered how she made it so straight, her sister's hair that she had never before seen hang free, at least not in daylight.

"That is good. You don't want to go inside. It is terrible."

"I won't. I don't want to."

Sadie fiddled with that large hoop of earring, a circle of silver metal like something that might be sold in a hardware store.

"You know one thing that completely boggles my mind?" Sadie said. "They can forgive the killer. They can forgive him, but they can't forgive me."

Katie shrugged. The baby Grace pressed her face into Katie's chest.

"It is not for us to understand, I suppose," she said.

Sadie stayed for three hours, three glorious customer-free hours, and then she left the baby with Katie as she went in that shockingly red rented car to fetch lunch.

"I'll just go down to the diner, get some takeout soup and sandwiches," Sadie said, braking at the edge of the road and calling through the open window as Katie stood on the porch with the baby. "Something warm. Comfort food."

Katie nodded. There was a bite of winter-to-come in the air. The baby was awake, gurgling like boiling soup. A bit of spit bubbled on her lips, and Katie wiped it with the sleeve of her dress.

As the car zoomed away, Katie went back into the warm with the baby. Grace was beginning to fuss, maybe knowing that her mother was gone. Katie jiggled her.

"Flex ties," she said, pointing to hardware hanging on pegboards, entertaining the baby. "Eye bolts. Nails, tubes, clamps."

Sadie returned with a big paper bag that smelled wonderful. She brought out with a flourish two Styrofoam bowls and she took off the lids, arranging the bowls on the counter like a waitress in a fancy place. Chicken corn soup, made just this morning, the chicken killed just last night. The soup floated golden with corn, hot broth steaming. Oh, how Katie loved chicken corn soup. It reminded her of being sick, and then getting better. Mother always made this when one of the children had a cold, when the kids were sick.

"Wow, have I missed this stuff," Sadie said. She produced two plastic spoons, and a napkin each, plus a bottle of iced tea for Katie and lemonade for herself.

"Bon appétit," she said. "That's French."

Sadie produced two more white foam containers: sandwiches, to go.

"Tuna for me, and BLT for you," she announced.

"You remembered," Katie said. "You remembered my favorite."

"How could I ever forget? Bacon, lettuce, tomato, bacon extra crunchy. Burned, even, to a crisp. Extra mayo, bread toasted. Ta-da!"

Katie stood by the counter, awkward, not quite sure what to do with the baby. Grace's eyelids, closed, almost transparent, were lined with purplish-blue veins. It was like a map, a tiny road map, that led to somewhere small and pretty.

"Oh," said Sadie. "She's sleeping. Hang on. I'll go get her car seat, so we can eat in peace."

Sadie left after lunch, leaving Katie with empty arms and an aching heart. Katie could actually feel the pain in her left chest as she watched the car until it disappeared down the road. Katie could still see the tire tracks in gravel, the place where Sadie parked. *Sadie drives a car. She dresses in worldly clothes. She is the mother of a baby, and she lives in New York. She has a telephone and a television and a computer and a job.* Katie could hardly believe what she has just seen, what her eyes have witnessed.

"Goodbye," Katie whispered to nobody in particular.

Katie hated goodbyes, especially when they involved her sister.

The schoolhouse was being demolished. It was Thursday, early, a misty morning before daybreak, and construction lights glared in the haze. Katie stood with her bicycle on the road, watching as a large monster of a backhoe rolled across the ground and tore into the overhang of the school porch. Then it knocked down the bell tower, toppled the walls, and there was nothing left. Just a pile of debris, crashed, where once had stood Nickel Mines School.

At least a dozen others – Amish and reporters – gathered on the road, watching. Nobody spoke, and Katie stayed until 7:30 a.m., when the dump trucks arrived and took away what remained.

There was nothing left, just a bare patch of earth, dirt, and Katie turned and pedaled away, heading for work.

It was five years later. Katie still lived at home and she still was not married, not yet. She was a spinster, an old maid schoolteacher. Probably she'd never get married, but that was all right. Perfectly all right with Katie.

Katie taught twenty-four children, two dozen wonderful children in grades one to eight, and she knew each child by heart. She memorized their faces and their full names and their favorite places to sit in the classroom. She purchased books with her own money, and she also bought special colored chalk – yellow and green and pink – for the board, and candy – peppermints and caramels – for rewards.

Katie was a teacher, a good teacher, and her mission was to be sure that each child learned, that every student enjoyed coming to school, that everybody was safe. Katie's job was to protect.

These are your lessons, young people. Learn your lessons and I will do my best to protect. I will do my best. I promise.

One day in October, a day when the sky seemed to hold more blue than usual, Katie rode her bicycle before school to Nickel Mines Hardware. Her plan was to purchase items for an art project that involved barn wood, and these are the things she bought: flex ties. Eye bolts. Nails, tubes, clamps.

Katie purchased these things for her classroom, for her children, so that she could teach them to make something beautiful. So that she could teach them that all things are useful, they really are, even the bad things, the ugly things, the things that make you stop dead in your tracks and shake your head.

"Have a good day," Katie said to the young woman working behind the register. The woman nodded briskly, tucked Katie's receipt in the brown paper bag, and she handed it to her. This girl, too, was efficient. Nickel Mines Hardware was lucky to have her.

"You, too," the girl said. "You have a nice day, too."

"Where's the dog?" Katie asked. "The German Shepherd named Jake?"

"Oh," said the young woman. "He died."

"Oh," said Katie. "Okay."

Katie took a big breath and then she left Nickel Mines Hardware, pedaling in the direction of the school, of her home, of her classroom. The students would soon be arriving. *The children, the children, the children; that's what mattered.*

Katie passed the United Methodist Church, a place she'd gone by a hundred times; more: a thousand times in her life. The milkman was buried here, in an unmarked grave in his wife's family's plot. There was a heart-shaped stone for the milkman's baby, the infant who died before she was born. Katie had read of this in the newspaper, and her family had been to the grave on that day, the morning of the shooter's funeral. The day that Katie could not, would not, attend to what she knew she should do.

But there was a time for everything, and to everything there was a season, and today, well, today was the day.

Katie pushed the foot brake on her bicycle pedal. She skidded to a stop, and then she turned around. She pedaled into the church parking lot, up the lane, into the cemetery, through the rows of stones. Katie knew where to look. There it was: the shiny heart-shaped grave with the stillborn baby's name. Katie, who so loved children, could only imagine that pain.

Katie laid her bicycle in the grass, and she knelt by the stone, reaching out and tracing the baby's name. Somewhere nearby, buried beneath the dirt, was what remained of the milkman. Ashes now, and bone.

That man, that tall and lean man with the hay-colored hair and the ordinary eyeglasses, was part of a family. *A family*. For the first time, Katie was struck like lightning by the thought that he was somebody's *husband*, somebody's *father*, somebody's *son*. He was somebody who was loved. If he was Amish, he would have been shunned, in life as in death. He was dead to them.

I, too, am imperfect, Katie thought. *Flawed. Sadie, too, and even my sweet little niece Grace. All of us.*

Katie picked up a fistful of cool dirt, and then she let it go. She released the clumps of earth onto the ground, scattering dirt around like flour on a pie crust, and Katie said out loud: "I forgive."

She said the words again, soft, a whisper that came from deep in her gut. "I forgive."

Her breath made a cloud before her face, a puff of spoken words into frosty air, and then it faded away.

Katie picked up her bag of items purchased from Nickel Mines Hardware and she straightened her bicycle, twisting the handlebars into the correct position, hitching up her skirts, and straddling the seat. She had work to do.

It was time to get to school, and Katie Zook had better pedal fast. *Hurry up. Get to work.* She had students to teach and a job to do, an honorable job, a good job, a good job, if she did say so herself.

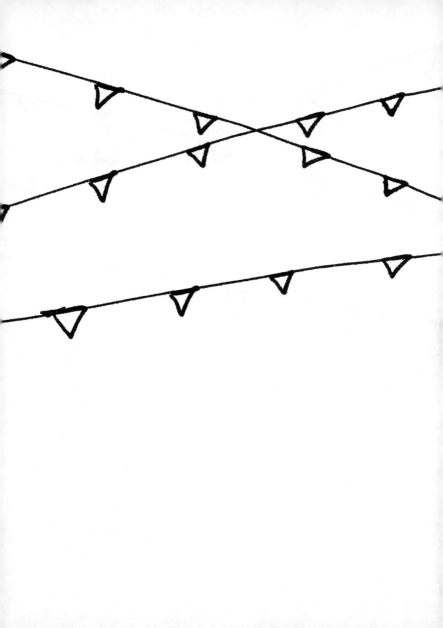

Acknowledgements

———

With special thanks to The Sunday Times
EFG Private Bank Short Story Award 2012
judges: Melvyn Bragg; Ian Hart; Andrew
Holgate; Hanif Kureishi; Joanna Trollope
and the non-voting chairman of judges, Lord
Matthew Evans. Thanks also to Keith Gapp of
EFG Private Bank and the Booktrust team.